I0592665

A Murderer's Music Box

By

Manuel Rose

And

Melissa Rose

$7.99
ISBN 978-0-692-16170-8
50799>

9 780692 161708

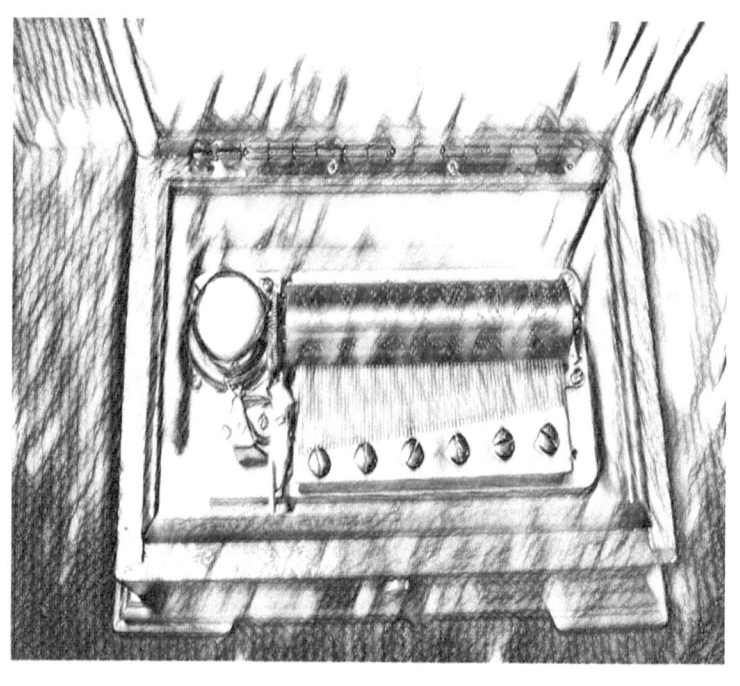

DEDICATION

I dedicate this book to my father who has been a constant source of love, support and inspiration since I was a child. Throughout the years, he and I have worked together as a team on countless creative projects. Although my father and I have been writing children stories for quite some time, he and I have always been fascinated by the thriller-horror genre. I started writing this particular story on my own many years ago, and then he developed it even further. We're both very excited by the results of our collaborative efforts, and we hope you enjoy this story just as much as we enjoyed writing and recording it together.

Published by MMR Productions
815 Route 82 # 51
Hopewell Junction, New York 12533

PUBLISHER'S NOTE
This is a work of fiction. Names, characters, places, and incidents either
are the product of the author's imagination or are used fictitiously,
and any resemblance to actual persons, living or dead, business
establishments, events, or locales is entirely coincidental.

Books, audio books and theme music soundtrack can be ordered.
For information please write to:
MMRproductions.com
815 Route 82 # 51
Hopewell Junction, New York 12533

CONTENTS

The Wellwoods are moving away from the chaos of the city and buying their first dream home in the country lands of upstate New York. Despite the odd behavior of the townsfolk, and being the first visitors in several years of one house in particular, the Wellwoods can't resist the lovely charms of the old, Colonial house and quickly make it their new home; that is, all except for their 12-year-old daughter, Samantha, who senses a malevolent presence in the house and wants nothing more than for her family to escape it! For the Wellwoods, their beautiful country dream turns into a ghastly nightmare when Samantha and her father find an old music box in the attic that harbors a sinister secret which soon brings turmoil, death and destruction to all occupants of the house. But all is not as it seems when the story unfolds…

If you found this book to be a riveting, hair-raising ride, then you're going to love our fully dramatized audio movie in audio book format available at:

Amazon.com
And for download on Audible.com

Theme from "A Murderer's Music Box" by Manuel Rose is available at
CDBaby.com

ACKNOWLEDGMENTS

I would like to thank my family for all the support in pursuing this entire project that has been 5 years in the making. To my daughter, Melissa, especially, for coming up with the idea, editing and helping with the narration of the audio book.

Manuel Rose

**Prologue**

I was almost 13 years old when I lost my mom and dad. After all these years, I still remember it as if it were yesterday. Something evil had taken them away from me, something evil in that house. My parents weren't prepared for what was to happen to them. They had no way of knowing.

To them, it was just a nice, quiet old house, out in the country, away from the city and away from everyone. I still get chills just thinking about it, and the nightmares that never end. If I hadn't escaped, I would have suffered the same fate as they did.

Chapter 1
The Wellwoods

The year was 1985. It was a dark and dingy Saturday morning in the middle of October. The sky was overcast, which made everything look eerie. A cold wind coming in from the north made it even worse. This was the day we were going to the real estate office to shop for a new home. I wish we never went. I wish I could just turn back the clock, and then maybe, just maybe, my parents would be alive today.

My mom and dad were tired of that cramped apartment in the city; they wanted to move out into the country. Mom and dad thought it would be a better place to raise children. My name is Samantha Wellwood. I was just your average 12-year-old girl with short black hair and pimples. Yeah, I had a lot of those. I didn't think I was beautiful or special. One other thing, at 5-feet-2-inches and being underweight, I was very petite. My parents and relatives always teased me about flying away in the wind.

Heather, my mom, was pregnant with another child. She was 38 years old and worried that it might be a risk for her age. Mommy was very pretty with her long light-brown hair. Even with her pregnancy, she still had a slender figure. I had mixed feelings about moving, missing my friends, starting in a new school, and trying to make new friends.

Michael, my dad, promised me he would get me my very own horse to ride, and that was my weakness. Every weekend we would drive upstate to the Scatskill Mountains and go horseback riding. It was a long drive, but I didn't mind. I loved horses. My dad and I would ride together while mom watched. Mom liked horses, but she was afraid of climbing up on one; she thought she might fall off and get hurt. My dad knew I was sad when it was time to go back home, he loved me more than anything in the world. I was daddy's little girl. Daddy was tired of New York City, the hustle and bustle, and the crowds. At 34-years-old, 6-feet tall and thin, my dad was very handsome. Daddy was a video producer; he produced his own how-to-videos and sold them through mail order. Since my dad's business was portable, moving wouldn't affect his income. Mom, on the other hand, was a doctor in a city hospital. She would have to commute every day, or work in a hospital somewhere else. Mom had made us blueberry pancakes with sausages for breakfast. We had just finished eating when dad made the announcement.

"Today will be different from every other Saturday. Yes, we will be going upstate, but this time we'll be looking for a new home in the country!

I'm sorry Samantha, but we won't have time to go horseback riding today," said daddy.

Knowing of my disappointment, he reminded me of his promise to get me my very own horse to ride, and then he turned to mom and said...

"Heather, did you make the appointment with the real estate agent?"

"Yes, Michael, I did. We have to be there at 12:30."

We each took our turn going to the bathroom, grabbed our coats and left. One thing good, we lived on the ground floor of an old 5-story house, so we didn't have to walk up or down any stairs. We followed daddy to the car.

"All right everyone, fasten your seat belts, and let's go house-hunting!" Daddy stated.

We were in the car heading north. It was an old, blue, four-door Sedan. Since the year was 1985, that made the car 10 years old, but daddy kept it in good shape. I loved watching my dad drive.

He looked so handsome, even though he was losing his dark-brown hair. Mom looked as pretty as ever sitting next to him. The drive upstate seemed to take forever, but the foliage was pretty. We drove up and down the mountains for over an hour. Dad was getting off at the highway exit called "Scatskill," when he announced...

"We're here everyone!"

Daddy parked the car, and we all got out.

Chapter 2
A New Home

Scatskill Realtors

The real estate office was right off of the highway exit and looked like an old house that was converted into an office. The lawn was balding and the bushes were overgrown. When we went inside, an old man with gray hair, beard, and glasses greeted us with a southern drawl.

"HOWDY FOLKS! Welcome to 'Scatskill Realtors!' I'm Bud Smith. What can I do fer you's?"

Bud was short, about 5-feet tall. He looked shorter than me, and his prominent belly and beard made him look like Santa Claus. My dad was the first to answer him.

"We're the 'Wellwoods.' We had a 12:30 appointment?" Daddy indicated.

"Oh, yeah, I remember, you're..."

"Michael Wellwood, and this is my wife, Heather."

"How do you do?" Mommy asked Mr. Smith.

"Howdy Ma'am. And who's this purdy little thing?"

"I'm Samantha."

"Samantha? Why that sure is a purdy name," Mr. Smith stated.

"Thank you, sir."

"Now folks, I've got just the house fer you's. It's about 10 miles north of here in 'Lightningville.' Now if y'all just hop in ma van, I'll take you's there," said Mr. Smith.

We followed him outside to this old, beat-up white van. It must have been over 20-years-old with plenty of rust to prove it. Mom and dad just looked at each other, bewildered.

"Now, folks, it may not look like much, but trust me, it'll get us there," Mr. Smith said with a smile.

We all got in Mr. Smith's ancient van and drove off to Lightningville. The road was full of twists and turns. The suspension in the van was so bad that we felt e-v-e-r-y bump, and let me tell you, there were plenty of bumps. I wish we went in our car. Finally, we were slowing down when Mr. Smith said...

"Folks, we're almost there, it's just up there on Horror Hill."

"Horror Hill?" Mommy and daddy asked in unison.

"Yep, Horror Hill."

"Why is it called 'Horror Hill,' Mr. Smith?" Mommy asked.

"Well...ya see ma'am...that there's a long story. I'll tell ya about it later. Right now, let's take a look at your new home!"

"That's if we buy it," mommy said.

"Of course, I just know you're gonna love it and the price is just right," Mr. Smith declared.

When we got up to the top of the long and winding hill, we saw this big, old, 2-story white Colonial house. It looked like no one had lived in it for years. No other homes were near it, a lone wolf, that's what it was, a lone wolf. There were overgrown vines all over it. The lawn looked like it was recently cut, although there were more weeds than grass in it. A new mailbox and post were recently installed. The house was waiting for new people to occupy it. I had a strange feeling about it. Mr. Smith drove us up the long, circular driveway and stopped at the top. He turned the motor off, but it continued to run a little bit before it finally stopped.

"This is it, folks!"

We all stepped out of the van. It was a big piece of property. Mom and dad were very impressed.

"Wow!" Daddy exclaimed.

"This is way out of our league, hon," mommy said.

"No it ain't. As I said, it's priced just right. Now come on folks, let me give ya the grand tour," Mr. Smith said as he waved his hand in the direction of the house.

Then, it started to rain.

"You folks got an umbrella?" Mr. Smith asked my parents.

"I'm afraid we left it in our car," daddy said with a guilty expression.

"Oh, that's just great dear, a lot of good it's gonna do us there!" mommy said with a twinge of anger.

"Sorry, dear."

"Eh-he-he...Now folks, no need ta start fightin' 'bout an umbrella! I got's a couple of umbrellas in ma van," Mr. Smith chuckled.

Mr. Smith went to get the umbrellas inside the van.

"Here ya go, folks!"

He each gave mom and dad an umbrella and kept one for himself. I stayed with daddy so I wouldn't get wet.

"Ok, folks. This here's about 10-acres of what usta be farmland; let's take a look. Now, Mr. Wellwood, I believe you mentioned something about keeping horses?" Mr. Smith asked.

"Yes, I did. I promised my daughter I'd get her a horse someday," daddy said as he smiled at me.

"Well, now you can, Mr. Wellwood. If y'all just take a look over yonder, you'll see the stables that can hold up to four horses."

"Wow! Daddy, look!"

"I see, I see."

"And this here's a two-car detached garage!" Mr. Smith eagerly stated.

"Mr. Smith, I really think this is out of our league. I told you over the phone that we couldn't spend more than $250,000 on a home," mommy nervously said.

"Ma'am I've been tellin' y'all along, it's priced just right."

"My wife's right, Mr. Smith. We couldn't possibly afford this. How much is it anyway?"

"Why, it's priced to sell at only $250,000, isn't that what you folks wanted to pay for a house?"

Mom and dad were shocked; they just looked at each other in bewilderment. Clearly the house and property were worth much more than that, but why was it so cheap? Something was terribly wrong here.

"Come on folks! Let's take a look inside the house!"

"Anything to get out of this rain," mommy miserably said.

As we approached the old house, the rain was getting worse. I really wanted to check out the stables. Suddenly, we smelled it, the most horrible stench in the world. It seemed to be emanating from behind the house. The giant backyard that led to the woods, smelled like death itself.

"Oh, God! What is that foul smell?" mommy exclaimed as she pinched her nose.

"It smells like a dead animal, or maybe a skunk," daddy said as he wrinkled up his nose.

"Yep, that's what it is all right, a dead critter," Mr. Smith stated as he nervously looked around.

There was a long, curved brick pathway that led to the front porch of the house. When we got there, I noticed a big cross that looked like it was burned into the front door. Mom pointed it out.

"What's with the cross, Mr. Smith?" she asked.

"Eh... religious folks, ma'am."

"We can always change the door, hon," daddy said.

"Oh, no! Ya don't wanna do that!" Mr. Smith exclaimed.

"Why not, Mr. Smith?" mommy asked.

"Well...ya see folks...that's kind of a good luck charm. Now, let's take a look inside."

Mr. Smith fumbled for the keys until he found the right one.

"There it is! Come on, folks!"

When we walked inside, we could tell that the house hadn't been occupied in years. There were cobwebs everywhere. We were standing in a big foyer, painted white, with a large chandelier and a dusty old mirror hanging on the right wall. Under the mirror, there stood a small, oval-shaped, dark-walnut colored, antique table. On the left wall, there was a portrait of a young man in a suit, holding what looked like an old-fashioned music box. The man had a big smile on his face. On the bottom of the portrait, there was a small brass plate; it had the name "Roger Thompson" engraved on it. Mom looked over at Mr. Smith.

"Who's he?"

"Oh, that's the feller that built this here place. Come on now, let me show y'all around. Now, at the end of this hallway, on the right, is a spacious kitchen."

The old wooden floors creaked with every step we took, until we walked into the kitchen. The kitchen had a black and white tile floor, mauve-colored wallpaper with floral patterns on it, and dark-walnut colored wooden cabinets. Dad fumbled for the light switch.

"Don't bother yourself, Mr. Wellwood, the juice is off. Been off for quite awhile now. Ya see, no one's lived here, ever since..."

"Ever since what, Mr. Smith?" mommy questioned.

"Aww...nothin' ma'am. Y'all ain't got no time ta listen ta some ole stories now."

"I'd like to hear about it, Mr. Smith!" Daddy exclaimed.

"Some other time, Mr. Wellwood. Now, before it gets too dark, let me look around for a lantern. I think there's an oil lantern in the pantry, let's see now...yep there it is!"

Mr. Smith went into his pocket and pulled out a cigarette lighter. He lit the lantern and went to the large, white porcelain sink on the other side of the room.

"Looky here, folks! Now, that there's what I call a kitchen sink, ya just don't see that kinda quality anymore. Today, all kitchen sinks are made outta metal. Of course, there isn't any water without the juice, that is."

"What?" Mommy asked.

"Why is that, Mr. Smith?" Daddy questioned.

"Well, ya see folks...this house has its own well and septic system."

"A well? You mean we've got to go outside and crank up a bucket for water?" Daddy asked.

"Oh, for God's sakes! No, folks, it's electric! There's a well pump about 200 feet in the ground that gives ya water. Since there's no electricity, there's no water."

"You also mentioned a septic system? What's that?" Daddy questioned.

"The septic system is your sewage system. You have a septic tank, which holds the solids and the leach field that drains the fluids. When you folks get ready ta move in, y'all can call the electric company ta put the juice back on. Now, over here's your stove and oven, it's electric also. There's no gas up here. And this here's your refrigerator. These appliances may look a little old, but rest assured, everything works. As you folks can see, there's plenty of cabinet space."

Lightning had started flickering outside, followed by a roar of thunder.

"I guess that's why it's called 'Lightningville,'" mommy laughed.

"Yeah, how 'bout that? Now around this corner, on the right, is the dining room."

The dining room was large and fully furnished. The walls were covered with dark wood paneling, which matched the wood floor. There was a beautiful chandelier hanging down from the ceiling. Over the right wall, there stood a beautiful light oak china hutch. In the center of the room, there was a matching rectangular table with six chairs. Mom and dad had a surprised look on their faces.

"Look, hon, there's furniture and everything!" Daddy exclaimed.

"I see it, but I don't believe it. Mr. Smith, you didn't tell us there was any furniture here!" Mommy stated.

"Why folks, the whole house is furnished! Come, let me show ya!"

We followed Mr. Smith out of the dining room and into the family room. It was a huge, rectangular-shaped room. There was a beautiful brick fireplace at one end. The room had dark oak wood flooring with an oval-shaped Oriental rug in the center to complement it. The family room was also fully furnished. There was a large, fancy sofa covered with dark-green cloth, and a matching love-seat. By the fireplace, there was an antique, dark, mahogany-colored wooden rocking chair.

"Wow! Honey, we don't have to buy any furniture!" Daddy beamed.

"But, Michael, what about the furniture we have at home?"

"That old stuff? Not too long ago, you were talking about getting new furniture. Remember…?"

"Yeah, but, Michael…"

"Well, now we don't have to. Besides, we don't have enough furniture in our apartment to fill this big house."

"Mr. Smith, you said the whole house was furnished?" Mommy questioned.

"That's right, ma'am."

"The bedrooms too?" Mommy asked.

"Everything."

"Can we see?"

"Sure! But first, let me show y'all one last room down here, then I'll take y'all upstairs, it's on the way." Mr. Smith led us back towards the other end of the house, past the hallway where the portrait of that strange man was hanging up. I didn't like that painting, there was something eerie about it. I wanted to rip that painting off of the wall and burn it. If we did move into this house, that's what I would do. "Roger Thompson" looked like a strange man...maybe even evil. When we got to the parlor, Mr. Smith spoke again.

"Folks, this here's the living room or what they use ta call the parlor, as y'all can see, it's as big as the family room."

It was. The living room had a parquet wood floor, cream-colored walls and was completely furnished. There was a large, floral-printed sofa against one wall. In front of the sofa, there was an oval-shaped mahogany cocktail table. On each end of the sofa, there were two matching end tables, each with matching antique brass lamps. There were also two floral-printed chairs in the room matching the sofa. Clearly, the person that lived in this house had a taste for fine antique furniture. It all just needed to be cleaned. My parents were awed.

"Well, what da ya think, folks?" Mr. Smith asked my parents.

"Nice, very nice!" Mommy exclaimed.

"Sure is!" Daddy said in agreement.

"Great! Now, come let me show y'all the upstairs."

We followed Mr. Smith out of the room towards the hallway again, until mom noticed three doors.

"Mr. Smith!"

"Yes, ma'am?"

"Are these closets?"

"One of them is. Here, let me show you. This here's a big walk-in closet."

"Nice!" Mommy said in amazement.

"And this is one of the bathrooms. This house has two-and-a-half bathrooms. There are two full baths upstairs, and the half bath downstairs."

"And what about this door, Mr. Smith?" Daddy asked.

"Oh, that door leads to the basement, Mr. Wellwood, it's unfinished, just the boiler down there. Would ya like ta see?"

"Sure!"

"Michael! I want to see the bedrooms first."

"All right, dear. Let's go upstairs first, Mr. Smith."

"Sure, folks! Whatever you say. Come on, I'll show you's the upstairs."

Mr. Smith took us up the curved staircase that creaked and squeaked with every step we took. When we got to the top, the first things we noticed were six closed doors. You would think as a real estate agent, Mr. Smith would want to keep all of the doors open in the house to air it out! All of the doors in this house were closed for a reason: either to keep something out, or to keep something in.

"Mr. Smith? Why are all the doors closed?" Mommy questioned.

"Sorry, ma'am, force of habit. I always close and lock everything up. Now, this door on your left, is the master bedroom."

The master bedroom looked more like a hotel suite than a bedroom. It was elegant with its plush, wintergreen wall-to-wall carpeting, matching draperies with light-green Venetian blinds and cream-colored textured wallpaper. The bedroom was almost as large as the living room downstairs. The master bedroom was fully equipped with its own full-sized bathroom, a large walk-in closet, and a linen closet. As far as furniture goes, it was all Colonial. A beautiful, walnut-colored, king-sized bed with large bedposts was standing against the entrance wall. There were also matching night stands with old-fashioned lamps on each end of the bed. A large dresser with a mirror and an armoire were against the opposite wall. Like Mr. Smith said, the house was completely furnished, but why? Why would anyone leave such beautiful furniture behind? It's as though the person that lived here before, had to leave in a hurry. The bed had been made, and there were towels in the bathroom. What were they running from?

Mr. Smith himself was looking uneasy, it's as if he wanted to leave. What was he hiding? A cold draft went right through me; it sent chills down my spine. I know Mr. Smith felt it too, but where did it come from? All of the windows were closed and locked. Something happened here, something terribly wrong, but what? Mr. Smith knew, but he wasn't saying anything, he just stood there with a frightened look on his face. He wanted to leave.

"Err—you folks seen enough?"

"Mr. Smith! Are you all right?" Mommy asked with genuine concern.

"Sure, ma'am, I'm just a little cold, that's all."

"Well, it is a little chilly up here," mommy told him.

"Come on, we better leave before it gets too dark and this here lamp runs out of oil," Mr. Smith said.

"But, Mr. Smith, we haven't seen the rest of the house!" Mommy exclaimed.

"He's right, hon, besides the way it's raining, the roads will get flooded in no time."

"Michael, I just want to see the other rooms up here!"

At that moment, Mr. Smith collapsed to the floor.

"Mr. Smith!!! Honey, do something!!!" Mommy shrieked.

"Heather, let's get him up on the bed!"

"Ok."

"I'll open the windows to give him some air," daddy said.

"Mr. Smith! Are you all right?!" Mommy shouted.

"I'll be fine, just let me rest a bit, and then we can go," Mr. Smith said in a weak voice.

"Michael, see if you can call for help on that phone!"

"Sure, hon! Hello? Hello?! The phone's dead."

"Like everything else in this house," mommy indicated with a twinge of frustration.

Remember, the year was 1985. Cell phones weren't popular yet.

"I'll be fine, folks. Just gimme a few minutes," Mr. Smith groggily stated.

"God, I wish there was something we could do for you, Mr. Smith," mommy said gently.

"Thank you, ma'am. I'll be ok."

"You said there's no water here, right?" mommy asked Mr. Smith.

"None whatsoever. Everything's turned off."

"Mr. Smith. Michael and I are really interested in this house, but we just want to see the rest of it before we make our decision. Would it be all right if we take a quick look around while you rest here? We promise not to take too long."

"Sure, folks, go right ahead. I'll be fine."

"Thanks, Mr. Smith. We'll leave our daughter here with you. If you need us, just give us a shout. Samantha! Stay here with Mr. Smith while we take a look around," mommy said.

"Mommm, do I have to?!"

"Yes, you do!"

"I wanna go with you guys."

"Samantha, please...it'll just be for a little bit, I promise," she said impatiently.

"Oh, all right. Please don't take too long."

"We won't. Come on honey," she called to dad.

"Yes, dear."

They left me alone with Mr. Smith while they checked out the other rooms. Daddy took the lantern and now it was getting darker, but I could still see Mr. Smith's face, the terror in his eyes. I decided to question him.

"Mr. Smith?"

"Yes?"

"Something happened here, didn't it?"

"Wadda ya mean?"

"You're hiding something, aren't you?"

"I don't know what you're talking about, girlie."

"My name is Samantha, Mr. Smith."

"I ain't hidin' nothin', Samantha. It's jes your imagination, that's all."

Then, he just lied there and stared at the ceiling. I couldn't wait for mom and dad to return. Just then, they did. Mom and dad seemed impressed by what they'd seen. I ran to them and cried.

"Mommy, daddy, can we go now?"

"Sure, honey, what's wrong?" Mommy asked.

"How's Mr. Smith?" Daddy chimed in.

"He's fine. Can we go now? Please?"

"You folks ready ta leave?" Mr. Smith interrupted. "Are you all right, Mr. Smith?" mommy asked him.

"Sure! Just needed ta rest a bit. We need ta go before the roads get flooded."

As we walked out of the room and into the hall, we heard it. A faint, haunting melody that seemed to be coming from beyond the door in the ceiling, it's as if it were calling us. The tune was hypnotic in every way, it wanted us to stay. Mr. Smith broke out into a cold sweat.

"Come on, folks!"

But mom wanted answers.

"What's that?"

"What, ma'am?"

"Well, don't you hear it, Mr. Smith? It sounds like music, like from a music box!" Mommy exclaimed.

"That's probably the wind, ma'am," Mr. Smith shrugged.

"That doesn't sound like the wind to me," she stated.

"Well, whatever it is, it's coming from up there. What's behind that door in the ceiling, Mr. Smith?" Daddy asked.

"Oh, that? That's just the attic."

"The attic? Why is it locked?" Daddy questioned Mr. Smith.

"Locked?"

"Yes! There's a padlock on it! Do you have the key, Mr. Smith?" Daddy asked.

"No, I don't."

"Mr. Smith. What's in the attic and why is it locked?" Mommy asked.

"Ah, folks, I dunno. I can only guess that the folks here before must have left some things up there they forgot."

My mom looked at him questionably.

"And you've never heard that before, or

found it strange that the attic was locked?"

"Ma'am, nobody's lived in this house for a long time. We don't get too many people looking at it either. Ya see, most folks wanna live near town. I jes come around every so often ta cut the grass and stuff."

Just then, the music stopped playing. It's as if someone or something had turned it off. That creepy, eerie little tune had just stopped, but why? Why did it play in the first place? All that was left now was the sound of the storm outside. Then came mommy's voice...

"It stopped! Did you hear that, Mr. Smith? It stopped!"

"Eh, probably the storm shook somethin' loose up there, ma'am. We really need ta leave folks."

I couldn't wait to get out of that house. Funny thing though, as soon as we left, the storm stopped. The drive back to the real estate office was a quiet one. No one said anything, not even Mr. Smith. All he did was wipe the sweat from his nervous face as he drove. He was the only one sweating, I wondered why.

Chapter 3
Back At The Office

When we got back to the real estate office, Mr. Smith pulled some papers out of his desk drawer.

"So wadda you folks think of the house?"

"Well, we know it needs a little work, Mr. Smith," daddy said.

"But the price is right," mommy smiled.

"You did say, $250,000. Right?" daddy asked.

"That's right, Mr. Wellwood. $250,000," Mr. Smith declared.

"Mr. Smith! You've got yourself a deal!" Daddy stated as he extended his hand to Mr. Smith to close the deal.

"No! Mom, dad, that place is creepy!"

"What do you mean, honey?" Mommy asked with a puzzled expression.

"Something bad happened there, I know it!"

"Ah, come on honey! That's ridiculous, how would you know? We've never been there before!" Daddy said as he looked at me.

"I just know, daddy. He's hiding something, aren't you, Mr. Smith?"

"Folks, I think your youngin' here is watchin' too much television. This here's a quiet area. Why there ain't nothin' goin' on in these parts, trust me."

"Mr. Smith's right, Samantha.

This is country, what could possibly go wrong here?" Daddy chuckled.

"Honey, it was just the storm playing tricks on you, that's all. Now, I think you owe Mr. Smith an apology," mommy sternly said to me.

"Mom!"

"That's no way to talk to a grown-up! Now, say you're sorry," she said to me again.

I bit my lip and apologized to him.

"It's all right, girlie," he said with a cheesy smile.

"I told you, don't call me girlie!"

"Sam!" Daddy yelled.

"Sorry."

"Honey, it's really a nice, old house. We even picked out a nice room for you!" Mommy smiled.

"And an office for me!" Daddy proudly said.

"There's even an extra room we could use for the baby," mommy said as she smiled at daddy.

"And another bathroom, plus an extra closet!" Daddy stated.

Mom and dad had obviously made up their minds. There was nothing I could say or do that would change that. They wanted that house, but I didn't.

"Samantha, as soon as we move in and unpack, I'll look around for a horse for you, just like I promised. All right?" Daddy winked at me.

"I can help y'all with that when yer ready."

"Would you, Mr. Smith?"

"Sure! I know just the place! Now, you folks able ta leave a deposit today?"

"Sure! How much do you need, Mr. Smith?" Daddy inquired.

"Ten percent will do folks!"

"Heather, write Mr. Smith a check please."

"Mr. Smith, before I do, there's just a couple of questions I'd like to ask you."

"Go right ahead, ma'am, shoot!"

"Well, for one thing, you were going to tell us why it was called 'Horror Hill?'"

"Well...like I said...that there's a long story. But ta make it short, Mr.
Thompson, the builder of that house, was sort of...different."

"You mean like, eccentric, Mr. Smith?" Mommy asked him.

"Yes, I believe that's what you'd call it. He was also very rich. Anyway, he didn't like too many folks around him. He really loved his privacy. Yep, peace and quiet was all he wanted. Mr. Thompson really didn't want too big of a house, just plenty of land, all to himself and family. He bought up all that land up there except the woods. That there's a protected area, owned by the townsfolk. Well, anyway, ta kinda scare people away, he named it, 'Horror Hill.' Well, it worked. Nobody came near the place, much less wantin' ta buy it. Lots of folks are superstitious about things like that, they won't admit it, but they are."

"Well, we aren't superstitious, Mr. Smith. Right, honey?" Daddy declared.

"Right! Oh, my!" Mommy exclaimed.

"You all right, hon?"

"Michael! I just felt the baby kick!"

"Really?"

"Why, yes! It's as if he or she were answering you."

"Ya see? Even your baby likes the house...ha ha ha!" Mr. Smith said with a cheesy laugh.

"Mr. Smith! How are the schools here?" Mommy asked.

"Why ma'am, best damn school district in the area. In fact, once y'all get registered, the bus will pick up your youngins right at the bottom of 'Horror Hill.' Err—any more questions?"

"Just one more, Mr. Smith, about how old is the house?" Mommy inquired.

"Well...let's see now... It was built in 1935, so that makes it 50 years old, but it's in good shape. The house had some updatin' about 15 years back."

"We've never done this before. This'll be our first house. Besides the deposit, what else do we have to do?" Mommy asked Mr. Smith.

"Why folks, y'all just leave that up ta ole Bud Smith. I'll handle everything for ya. I know a good lawyer that'll give y'all a good price. And I know which banks are givin' the lowest interest rates on mortgages. Eh...you folks got good jobs?"

"My wife here is a doctor."

"Oh, goody! Now, I'll know who ta turn to when I get sick...eh-eh-eh. And you, Mr. Wellwood, wadda you do?"

"I'm a video producer."

"Really? You do anything fer television?"

"No, I do How-To videos."

"Well, I don't think y'all will have a problem bein' approved. When y'all are ready, I'll set you's up with the closing. Congratulations, future homeowners!"

Mr. Smith got up from his desk to shake my mom and dad's hands. He was smiling all the while, but I saw right through that phony smile. There was something he wasn't telling us. Something, but what?

Chapter 4
Moving-In Day

Mom and dad woke me up early that Saturday morning in December. I was still tired, didn't get much sleep. I kept having bad dreams about the house, Mr. Smith, and that man in the picture. Thompson. Yes, that was his name. Roger Thompson. This was the day I dreaded. After two months, we were finally moving into that house, that creepy old house on Horror Hill. Mom and dad were excited, but I wasn't. They couldn't see that there was something really wrong about that house. My parents sold all of our furniture to the building Superintendent, so we were able to sleep on our old beds one last time. All we were taking with us were our clothes, some appliances, my toys, and daddy's video equipment. He had plenty of that stuff. Christmas was only two weeks away. Mom couldn't wait to have the family over our new house for the holidays. Suddenly, there was a knock on the door.

"Who is it?" Mommy asked.

Mommy answered the door. It was our next-door neighbor and good friend, Maria.

"Maria! Come on in!" Mommy smiled.

"Oh, Heather, I'm gonna miss you guys," Maria said as the tears welled up in her eyes.

"We're gonna miss you too, Maria," mommy said as she wrapped her arms around her.

Maria was very pretty with her long blond hair and blue eyes. She used to be a model and she still had a great shape at 49-years-old, but at 5-feet tall, I was now taller than her.

"Where's my little princess?" Maria asked in reference to me.

"She's here. Samantha!" Mommy shouted.

"Yeah, mom?"

"It's Maria! Come here!"

"Hi, Maria!"

I gave her a big hug. I could see she was crying.

"What's the matter, Maria?" I asked her.

"Oh, I'm gonna miss you so much. My God, you're getting so big and beautiful. I remember when you were born."

"We'll come visit you. Won't we, mom?"

"Sure, we will! I've got to drive back and forth to work every day. The hospitals up there don't pay as much as the city. Besides, I'm not giving up my seniority."

"But, Heather, that's a long drive! You're gonna need a new car," Maria said with concern.

"I know!" Mommy stated.

"You don't know what the winters are like up there. They get more snow than we do," Maria continued.

"I know. We'll deal with it. Maybe, we'll get something with four-wheel drive," mommy told her.

"You're better off with a truck," Maria declared.

"No, I don't want anything that big. I want something small," mommy said.

"So, Heather, where's Michael?"

"He's bringing some stuff out to the van we rented," mommy said.

Just then, daddy walked through the door.

"Hello, Blondie!" Daddy smiled at Maria as he gave her a big hug. "How are you, Maria?"

"Why are you taking them away from me? Just kidding. I know you guys want your own house, but I'm gonna miss you all so much," Maria said again as a tear ran down her cheek.

"And we're gonna miss you too, Maria," daddy smiled.

"Maria, where's Ritchie?" mommy asked.

Ritchie was Maria's husband.

"He went to Florida to visit his mother. She's sick," Maria indicated.

That was real convenient for her. Now she could spend more time with her lover. I liked Maria a lot, I just didn't like what she was doing. My father and I were in the park when we saw her kissing a strange man, while her husband was at work. Another time, we caught them kissing in the hall. Daddy told me not to say anything to anyone about it, not even to mom. He said it wasn't our business.

"I'm sorry to hear that, Maria. What's wrong with Ritchie's mother?" Heather asked.

"She's got cancer, and it's spreading really fast."

"Oh my! Poor Ritchie!" Mommy said sympathetically.

My dad sat down, I know he felt bad, not only for Ritchie, but for himself. Daddy had just lost his mom to pancreatic cancer.

"Well, I know you guys have a lot to do, so I'm gonna go," Maria said.

Maria gave everyone a hug and left. Daddy was taking one last look around.

"I think we got everything."

"Are you sure, honey?" Heather asked.

"Yep," daddy said.

"All the boxes and suitcases?" Heather asked.

"Yep," Michael said.

"All of our clothes?" Mommy asked.

"Yep," daddy said.

"My toys, daddy? Did you pack all of my toys?"

"Yes, everything's packed."

"You should have thrown some of that stuff out. She's getting too big to be playing with toys," mommy said with a stern look.

"MOM!"

"Ah, honey. Let her have them, besides, we can always use some of that stuff for the baby," daddy said.

"Daddy!"

"I'm gonna miss this place," mommy sighed.

"I'm not," daddy said as he shrugged his shoulders.

"Oh, Michael, how can you say that? We've lived here for over 14 years!"

"Don't remind me," daddy scowled.

"Michael!"

"Oh, Heather, don't get me wrong. We've had some good times here, but it's time for us to move on. Ok, is everyone ready?"

"I'm ready," mommy mumbled as her arms were folded across her chest.

"I don't wanna go, daddy!"

I just broke down and cried in his arms.

"Aw...honey. It'll be all right, you'll see. I promise," daddy said as he tried to comfort me.

"All right, daddy."

"You wanna ride with me in the van?" Daddy asked me.

"Uh-huh."

"All right. Heather! You take the car and we'll follow you in the van. You remember how to get there?"

"Sure! You take the parkway all the way up and get off at Lightningville."

"Right. Now let's get going. It's already 2:00 and we still have to stop off and give the super the apartment keys," daddy said.

Dad gave the super the keys and we left. Daddy and I followed mommy upstate. She wasn't used to driving long distances, but she was gonna have to get used to it now.

"Holy shit! Did you see that?!" Daddy exclaimed.

"It was a deer, daddy! A real deer!"

"Jesus," daddy sighed.

Mommy had missed it, but daddy almost hit it. The big deer ran across the parkway and into the woods.

"Are you all right, Sam?" Daddy asked me.

"Yes, daddy."

"It was a buck," he said.

"A buck?"

"Yeah, a male deer."

"But, how do you know, daddy?"

"Well, you see honey...a buck has antlers, like 'Rudolph.' A doe, the female deer, doesn't have them."

I knew the difference between a buck and a doe, but I wasn't gonna tell him that. I was his world, and I knew he was sad. I was becoming a teenager next week. Six months ago, he became so depressed when I got my first period, that was right after his mother died. All daddy kept saying was, "my mom's gone and my baby's growing up." Now, mom's six months pregnant, it all happened at the same time. Mom didn't really want another child this late in her life, but he did. And now that house, oh God, I hated that house. We were almost there now, after an hour and a half of driving, we were getting off at the exit. Daddy was excited.

"Look, Sam, we're here!" After a few miles, we followed mommy up the driveway. Then, it started to snow.

"Look, daddy, it's snowing!"

"We better hurry up and unload the van so I can bring it back."

Mom got out of the car and told daddy we better hurry before the snow sticks.

"I know. I didn't hear anything about this in the forecast, did you?" Daddy asked.

"City forecast, Michael. It's like Maria said, they get more snow up here. Let's unpack the van so we can return it, all right?"

"You read my mind, dear. Come on Samantha, give me a hand with some of this stuff, don't pick up anything too heavy," daddy said.

Daddy didn't let me or mommy pick up anything heavy. We unloaded the van and headed back to the city. This time, I rode with mom to keep her company. It wasn't snowing in the city, just upstate. After we dropped off the van, we stopped off at the local pizza parlor. Daddy loved pizza and so did I. Daddy told us to eat fast because he was worried about driving in the snow. The roads upstate were bad. Snow had accumulated and was very slippery. It took us over two and a half hours to get back.

"Whew! We finally made it, I'm tired. It's already 10 p.m.," said daddy.

"We're all tired, dear. We'll unpack in the morning. Let's just wash up and go to bed," mommy stated.

"I'm with you, hon."

The house was all covered with snow. It was dark and cold outside, but I didn't want to go in, not in that house. We went to the front door, the one with the cross burned into it. Daddy took out the key, opened the door and flipped on the light. Nothing happened, no light.

"Ah shit!"

"What's wrong, Michael?"

"There's no light! Didn't you call the electric company?" Daddy asked.

"Yes, Michael, I did. They said they would turn it on by Friday."

"Yeah, well, that was yesterday, and it's not on," daddy said sternly.

"Maybe it's the bulb. Let's go inside, it's cold out here," mommy said shivering.

We went inside and mom took out a

flashlight that she kept in her purse. She looked around for another light switch and flipped it on, but it didn't work either. Nothing in that house worked. Mom and dad were pissed.

"I can't believe it, Heather. They probably won't come out till Monday. The whole weekend without electricity!"

"It's a good thing we ate in the city," mommy said with a twinge of nervousness in her voice.

"Yeah, right," daddy frowned.

"Look, we'll deal with it. Let's just wash up and go to bed," mommy sighed.

"Huh, you're forgetting something, dear. Everything in this house is electric, including the water."

"Shit! This is all your fault!" Mommy hissed at him.

"My fault?"

"You left everything up to me!"

"Stop it! Stop fighting!" I screamed.

I hated to see them fight, especially over that house, that damn house. Mr. Smith had the cleaners over to clean the house, but mom replaced all the linen on the beds anyway. We all took our turns in the bathrooms, knowing we couldn't flush. None of us used the bathroom downstairs, I think we forgot about it. Mom and dad tucked me in with extra quilted blankets to keep me warm, after all, it was cold and there was no heat. I didn't want to sleep alone in that house, but they made me. They told me I had to get used to my new room. I couldn't sleep. I tried, but I just couldn't sleep. All of a sudden, I heard it! That creepy, eerie little tune again. The tune we heard last time when we were here, two months ago. I turned to look at my clock on the nightstand, it lit up when I pressed the button.

It was only 1:00 in the morning. The music was getting louder. Then, I heard a child-like voice singing along with it in the background. I heard a voice whispering, I couldn't tell what it was saying, I was scared. Then, there were footsteps. The voice got louder, coming towards my door. I got up and went to the door, and slowly opened it to see if my parents were in the hallway. They must have heard it by now. My father was standing in the hallway, looking up at the attic door in the ceiling. Daddy looked like he was in a trance. Mom had left the oil lamp on in the hallway in case I had to go to the bathroom during the night. The voice was more pronounced now. I could hear what it was saying: "Let me out," "Let me out," chanting over and over again. My father was reaching up to the ceiling, he grabbed the attic door and pulled on it, but the padlock was still on it. I whispered to him: "daddy," I said, but he was hypnotized by that thing up in the attic.

Finally, I got the strength to yell at him.

"DADDY!"

"Samantha? What am I doing here, and what are you doing up?"

I grabbed and hugged him so tight with all my might, then I broke down and cried.

"Oh, daddy, please let me sleep with you and mommy, please, please, please!"

"Shhh, okay, okay. Let's not wake mommy up. We should be sleeping. This has got to be a dream."

"No, it isn't, daddy. Don't you remember? It was the music, daddy! The music brought you out here!"

"Music? What music?"

Daddy had no clue as to why he was in the hall that night. He didn't even remember leaving his bed, to him, it was just a dream, a very bad dream. I've never seen daddy look like that before. He was possessed by something, something evil in that attic. When we returned to the master bedroom, we found mommy still sleeping. She was in a deep sleep, snoring and everything. I squeezed in between mommy and daddy in that big, king-sized bed and fell asleep.

Chapter 5
The Attic

The next morning, mommy woke up from a nightmare.

"No!" she gasped. "Samantha? What are you doing here?"

"Huh?" I said in the middle of a yawn.

"Why aren't you in your room?"

"I was scared, mommy."

"You're almost 13-years-old. You should be sleeping in your own room."

"Hey," daddy said through a yawn. "Can't a guy get some sleep around here?"

"I'm sorry, dear. It's just, well, I had a bad dream, no, it was more like a nightmare, and now Samantha. Did you know she was sleeping here with us?"

"I know now!"

"Daddy! Don't you remember?"

"Remember what?"

"Last night, the music and the voice. Didn't you hear it, daddy?"

"Samantha! Did you say music and a voice?" Mommy asked.

"Yes, mommy, last night, it was coming from the attic."

"That was part of my dream!" Mommy exclaimed.

"Aw, come on you two," daddy said with disbelief.

"That wasn't a dream, mommy, that was real, and daddy was in the hall trying to open the attic door."

"He was?" Mommy asked with wide eyes.

"I was not. Listen, the two of you obviously had a bad dream, that's all," daddy said with a shrug.

"But, Michael, the same dream? How is that possible? Samantha, do you remember what the music sounded like?"

"Uh-huh. It was the same creepy music we heard the last time we came here," I said as a shiver crept up my spine.

"Like from a music box?" Mommy asked.

"Uh-huh."

"And you said it was coming from the attic?" Mommy asked.

"Yup."

"Michael! Today, I want you to check out that attic, see what's up there!"

"But, hon! There's a padlock on it, and we never got the key!"

"Well, then, we'll have to cut it. It's our house now," mommy declared.

"No, it ain't. For the next 30 years, it belongs to the bank," daddy chuckled.

"Michael!"

"Oh, all right, honey. After breakfast, we'll go to the hardware store and pick up a bolt cutter," daddy laughed again.

"Well, we'll have to go out for breakfast. I can't cook here, remember?" Mommy stated in mild anger.

"I know. We don't have any electricity, and the stove is electric," daddy said as he rolled his eyes.

I didn't want them to open up the attic, but there was nothing I could do to stop them. After all, I was just a kid. Do whatever I'm told to do and don't talk back, that's how I was raised. We went into town and stopped in the local diner for breakfast. It was a quaint, old-fashioned diner. The name on the front window said "The Happy Diner." There was a menu left on the table for us to look at. A short, thin, middle-aged waitress with black hair greeted us at the table.

"Good morning and welcome to the 'Happy Diner!' May I take your order?" she asked.

"We're undecided. Everything on this menu looks good," mommy stated.

"You folks new in town?"

"Why yes, we just moved into our new home!" Mommy smiled.

"Really? Well, congratulations!"

"Thank you," mommy said.

"Are you folks nearby?"

"Only a couple of miles up on Horror Hill," mommy casually said.

The waitress's smile turned into a frown.

"Horror Hill? Why would anyone wanna live there?" she said with panic in her voice.

"Why do you say that?" Daddy asked.

"Haven't you folks heard all the stories about that place?"

"No? We're from the city," daddy said.

My mother was getting upset. Mom looked at the waitress with fear in her eyes.

"What stories, Miss?"

"Well, don't mind me. It's just that, well, nobody's lived there in years. As a matter of fact, they've had trouble selling the place after what happened there."

"Anna!" A voice rang out in the distance.

"Excuse me, it's my boss."

"I wonder what that was all about, Michael!"

"I don't know, Heather, but I'd sure like to find out."

The waitress never came back, instead, a new waitress came in her place. Mom and dad asked the new waitress what happened to the other waitress. The lady said she had an emergency and had to leave. The waitress also said she was new in town, and didn't know anything about the area, or Horror Hill. My parents knew something was wrong, considering, they haven't even mentioned Horror Hill to the new waitress yet. After breakfast, we went to "Lightningville Hardware" across the street to get the bolt cutters. The hardware store was small and looked like it had been there for years. Mom and dad asked the clerk about our house. The old man just stared at them, before he answered.

"You folks livin' up there?" The clerk asked.

Daddy was next with the questions.

"Is there something you wanna tell us, sir? Did something bad happen up there?" Daddy asked.

"Good heavens, why do you say that, mister?"

"We get the impression that everyone around here is hiding something about the place we just bought."

"I'm sorry you feel that way, mister, I don't know anything, and I don't care to. It's none of my business. Now, what can I get you?"

My father purchased a hacksaw from the clerk, since he didn't have any bolt cutters. Dad knew it would be more work with the saw, but he was determined to get into the attic. On the way out, the clerk told us to be careful and good luck. The store clerk knew all about our house, but he wasn't saying shit about it. On the way back to the house, mom and dad talked about how strange the people in town were. Everything was fine, until you mentioned Horror Hill. Dad got the ladder from the basement and asked me to hold it for him under the attic door.

"Ok, Samantha. Hand me the hacksaw please," daddy said.

"Daddy, do you really have to open it?"

"Yes! It's time to see what's up in the

attic. Now, will you please pass me the hacksaw?"

"Ok, daddy, here," I said worried.

"Thank you."

Daddy started sawing the padlock off the attic door until it finally broke free.

"Whew! It was tougher than I thought."

Daddy climbed down the ladder with the broken padlock in his hand.

"Ok, Samantha, let's move this ladder out of the way. Now, watch your head. There's no telling what might come down when I pull on this handle. All right?"

"Yes, daddy."

Daddy pulled on the door handle in the ceiling, and down came the attic stairs.

"Cool! Pull-down stairs!" Daddy exclaimed.

He unfolded the rest of the steps and looked up.

"I guess we won't be needing this ladder anymore, Samantha. Give me the flashlight."

"Here, daddy."

"All right. Let me check it out. You stay here in case I need you."

"Yes, daddy."

Daddy climbed up the steps to the attic while I watched from below.

"Samantha!"

"Yes, daddy?"

"There's nothing but boxes up here. Come on up and help me go through them."

"Daddy, I'm scared. Can't mommy help you?"

"She's taking a nap. Please, it's all right, trust me."

I didn't wanna go up there, but he needed me, so like a good daughter, I went. The attic was like a warehouse, wall-to-wall boxes neatly stacked everywhere. Each box was bearing the name: "Thompson Music Box Company." It was cold up there. The attic was finished, but there was no furniture, only boxes. There was walnut colored wood paneling on the walls, (what little you could see of them). There were two windows, one on each end. The floor was covered with light-brown carpet, it was dark and musty up there. Cobwebs were everywhere.

"You see, Samantha? There's nothing to be afraid of here. Let's start opening up these boxes."

Daddy started to open up one of the boxes, while I held the flashlight.

"Wow! Look at this! Isn't that pretty?" He asked in amazement.

"Uh-huh," I said still nervous.

It was a beautiful, golden-brown, old-fashioned wooden music box, the largest music box I've ever seen! It was about the size of two hard cover books stacked together. The top of the music box was imprinted with gold lettering that read:

"Quality Crafted By Thompson Music Box Company."

When we opened the lid, there was a glass top, and there was a fancy golden movement underneath. The front of the box had a gold button with fancy engraved scrolls around it. On the bottom of the box, there was a large key with a tag tied to it. The tag said: "Handcrafted Quality By Thompson Music Box Company, Model number 135, Made In America."

"Let's wind it up."

Daddy wound up the music box, but it didn't play.

"Maybe you have to push this button on the front, daddy."

"Ok, let's try it."

Just then, joyful music started playing.

"That's the best sounding music box I've ever heard," daddy beamed.

It was the nicest sounding music box I've ever heard, too. It played beautifully, and I enjoyed watching the golden movement. The rotating cylinder with its pegs was plucking against the teeth of a metal comb. It looked like a miniature player piano, and it sounded like a symphony. The music box was unique in every way, being large and quite heavy. I would only guess to say the music box was worth well over $1,000. Then, all of a sudden, it stopped. The music had just stopped playing.

"What happened, daddy?"

"I don't know. Maybe you've got to press the button again."

Daddy pressed the button on the music box again. This time, it played a different tune. We were amazed. We've never heard a music box play more than one tune before; not only that, it seemed to play complete melodies, not just excerpts of them. Daddy and I watched and listened to the beautiful music coming from this little wooden box. But after a while, the music stopped again, just like before.

"Press it again, daddy! Please?"

"Sure, Samantha!"

Daddy pressed the button on the box again. Once more, the box played a different tune. All in all, the music box had played three complete melodies. I must admit I was really intrigued by it. How could something so beautiful, so harmless, pose a threat to me? But there was something evil up there, we just didn't find it yet. It was waiting patiently, for the right time.

"Do you like it, Samantha?"

"Yes, daddy, I do."

"Here, you can have it. Put it on your dresser in your room."

"Oh, thank you, daddy!"

I gave him a hug and a kiss. Daddy told me not to wind it too tight and don't drop it. I helped him open up some more boxes until mommy started calling us.

"Michael! Samantha!"

"We're up here, mommy!"

"You guys are still up there?"

"Yeah, mommy, and we found some cool stuff!"

"Really? Well, you can show me later. I'm hungry, let's go and get some food."

"What time is it, Heather?"

"According to my watch, it's 8:30, I can't believe it's that late."

"Wow! We've been up here all day? Ok. Let's go, I'm hungry, too."

"So am I, daddy."

After going through almost half of the boxes up in the attic, we went out to eat. There were over a hundred cases of music boxes up in the attic; it was going to take some time to go through them. The most disturbing thing was that none of those music boxes sounded anything like the one we've heard at night. We went back to The Happy Diner for dinner. This time, we never mentioned Horror Hill to anyone. Daddy and I had a cheeseburger deluxe, while mommy had fish. After we finished eating, we went to the nearby grocery store. Mommy wanted to get some bottled water to flush the toilets, "the stench was getting unbearable," she said. We didn't get home till 11:30. That night, I was awakened by the mysterious, eerie, creepy music again. I looked at the clock, it was

1:00 a.m. Again, I heard the children singing, the voice, and my father's footsteps. This was really freaking me out. I opened my door to find daddy staring up at the attic door, he was in a trance again. The voice was calling him, "let me out, let me out, let me out," over and over it chanted. This time, daddy pulled down the attic stairs and was going up. I ran and grabbed his arm.

"DADDYYY! NOOOO!"

"Huh? Samantha? What happened?"

"Oh, daddy!" I sobbed.

"What are we doing here?" he asked with genuine confusion.

"It was calling you again, daddy!" I continued to sob.

"What? What was calling me?"

"I don't know, I don't know!" I broke down again.

"Shhh. It's all right. It's all right, baby."

"Come on. You can sleep with mommy and daddy again. Ok?"

"Ok," I said through my tears.

I squeezed in bed between mom and dad again and fell asleep. The next morning, mommy woke up again from a nightmare.

"Michael, no!" she screamed.

"Wh-what! Honey, are you all right?" daddy asked in bewilderment.

"You tried to kill me!"

"What?!"

"In my dream, you tried to kill me."

"Oh, honey, it was just a dream. Go back to sleep," he said trying to comfort her.

"Not so fast! Young lady, I know you're up. What are you doing here again?

"I was scared and daddy said I could sleep with you."

"Michael?"

"Don't drag me into this. I'm just trying to get some Z's," daddy said with a yawn.

"Daddy! You've got to remember, please! Think, daddy, think! The attic, daddy. The attic!" I said sobbing.

"The attic?"

"Yes, daddy, the attic, you were going up there and I stopped you."

"Yes, yes, I remember now."

"Well, tell me, what were you doing up in the attic last night, Michael?"

"I—I don't know. All I remember is being on the attic stairs with Samantha."

"There's something strange going on around here," mommy said as she looked all around her.

"It's this house, mommy!"

"I think the cold air is getting to us. Michael, why don't we all check into a motel for a couple of days, just until the electricity gets turned on."

"Oh...I don't know," daddy said hesitantly.

"Michael, this is unhealthy! There's no

heat, no water! Christ, we can't even take a bath!"

"Oh, all right, but tomorrow's Monday. First thing in the morning, we call the electric company, all right?"

"All right, Michael. Now, let's pack some things and get going."

I was thrilled. I knew I could get a good night sleep away from that house. Now I wouldn't have to worry about my father and the attic, at least for a couple of days. The sun was out and since it was a little warmer, the snow started to melt on the driveway. Daddy was happy because it made it easier to drive. He knew he was going to have to get a snow thrower. The motel was plain, but nice, and it was near the Happy Diner. It was called "Lightningville Motor Inn." Everything around here, except the Happy Diner, seemed to be named after the town, "Lightningville." A middle-aged man with black hair and an English accent greeted us at the counter.

"Good morning! May I help you?"

"We're looking for a room for about two days," daddy said.

"Two nights?" The motel clerk asked.

"Yes, that should be fine. It's just until they turn the power on in our house," daddy told him.

"We have room #10 on the second floor available. It has two double beds and a refrigerator."

"That'll be fine," daddy said.

"Just fill out this registration form, and I'll need a major credit card."

"Ok."

When daddy handed the clerk back the form, the man took one look at it, and was shocked.

"My word, is that where you live?" The clerk asked with wide eyes.

"Yes, is that a problem?" Mommy asked.

"Oh, no, madam, I'm just surprised that someone finally bought the place, you see..."

"I know, no one's lived there in years," daddy said sarcastically.

"Precisely!"

"Mister, are you English?" I asked with a smile.

"Why, yes, young lady. I've lived in England all my life, except for the last 10 years or so. Ferguson! Show these fine people to their room, please."

"Sure, sir. Right this way, please," the bellhop said.

The bellhop was a short, overweight, elderly, black man. He was the first black person we've seen around here. The bellhop took us to the room. The room had two double beds, a TV, and a small refrigerator, just like the man said. It was nice to be able to bathe again, and sleep in a warm, cozy bed, away from that house. I slept in the same bed with mommy. Daddy slept in the other bed. I finally fell asleep and started dreaming, but I didn't know whether or not it was reality or just a dream. It seemed so surreal. I saw this man driving in a white van. The van said, "Conservative Power & Gas." He was driving down the road towards our home. All of a sudden, he saw this image of a man with a music box in front of him, but his face was distorted. That same creepy tune was playing, that tune we heard in the house. A blood-curdling scream erupted from the man's lungs. He tried to escape the ghastly image of the distorted figure. He heard it laughing and mocking him. Terrified, he slammed on the gas pedal, trying to escape. He went so fast, the van become airborne and flew passed our backyard and splashed into the lake. Furiously, he tried to unbuckle his seatbelt, but his heart succumbed to fear. I woke up in a cold sweat and found mommy on the phone with the power company.

"Conservative Power & Gas, may I help you?" the power rep asked.

"Yes, I was wondering why our power was never turned on," she said irritated.

The man talked so loud, and since I was near mommy, I heard almost every word he said.

"Where do you live, ma'am?"

"1 Horror Hill, in Lightningville."

"Excuse me, did you say 1 Horror Hill in Lightningville?"

"Yes."

"My God! He never made it!" the power rep exclaimed.

"Obviously, we have no electricity!"

"Ma'am, he was dispatched to your address on Friday morning and he never returned. We tried to get him on the radio but...excuse me, could you please hold?"

"Sure."

"Ma'am, they just found his body in the company van, at the bottom of Grace Lake!" the power rep said in horror.

"Oh, my God! I'm sorry."

"Ma'am, Grace Lake is right near your property. I won't be surprised if the police come by to ask you some questions."

"The police? Where did you say he was found?"

"Grace Lake, a local fisherman found the van there yesterday."

"I don't know of any lake by our property. We're new here," mommy nervously said.

"It's right passed the woods, ma'am. At any rate, are you home now?"

"No! We're in a motel. We're going back tomorrow."

"Ok. We'll send another man out there today.

I'm sure the police will be in the area."

"Thank you."

"Just let us know where you're staying in case there's a problem."

Mom gave the man the information, hung up the phone, and looked at me sternly.

"You heard everything, didn't you, Samantha?"

"Uh-huh." "It's not nice to listen in on grown ups' conversations. You were practically right on top of me!"

"I'm sorry, mommy."

At that moment, I realized that what I had was not just a mere dream, it was a premonition...suddenly, daddy just woke up from a bad dream, too.

"Nooo! You can't make me! Huh?"

"Michael! Are you all right?"

"Oh, what a horrible dream!" he said as beads of sweat erupted from his forehead.

"What was it about?" Mommy asked him.

"Something about the attic, Heather...someone or something up there wanted me to..."

"To do what, Michael?"

"Nothing. I guess it's my turn to have bad dreams."

"I guess you didn't hear me on the phone with the power company," mommy said.

"No. What did they say, Heather?"

"It seems that we've missed all the excitement when we left yesterday."

"What excitement?"

"The man from the power company, the one that was going to turn on our lights..."

"What about him?"

"He was found dead near our house."

"What? Where?"

"At the bottom of some lake."

"I didn't know we had a lake near us."

"Neither did I, and the way the power company has it, well, they think we have something to do with it."

"What?"

"Michael, I think we should head back home today."

"Yeah, I think you're right hon. It doesn't look good that we left right away. And the fact that we're the only people up there...there are no other houses nearby," daddy said.

"But mom, dad!!!"

"Your mother's right, Samantha, let's pack."

"All right everyone, but before we go, let me call the phone company, I forgot to do that," mommy stated.

"Yes, please do, I thought you did that a long time ago," daddy said in frustration.

"There's only so much I can do, Michael! You know, you can help out, too!" Mommy shouted.

"You make it sound like I do nothing!"

daddy yelled.

"Mom, dad, please don't fight."

"Look...let's just pack and head back," daddy said.

"Right," mommy said in response.

In the car, mom and dad talked about the attic. Dad wanted mom to help unpack the stuff up there. Mom said when the power was turned on, she would help with the attic, but she had to be careful.

"I'm pregnant," she said. "There's only so much I can do."

Chapter 6
<u>The Police</u>

We were pulling up the driveway when we noticed the police patrol cars. There was also a tow truck with a white van hooked up to it, and an ambulance. Daddy stopped the car. As we were getting out, a heavy-set, balding man in a suit approached us.

"You folks live here?"

"Yes, we do," dad answered.

"I'm detective Rosa, Homicide, and you are?"

"Michael, Michael Wellwood, and this is my wife, Heather, and my daughter, Samantha."

"How do you do?" Detective Rosa asked.

"How do you do, sir?" Mommy responded.

"You folks know what happened here?"

"Only what the power company told my wife over the phone," daddy stated.

"And what did they tell you, Mrs. Wellwood?"

"They told me that one of their employees, the man that was supposed to turn on our electricity, crashed into the lake," mommy said.

"That's right, ma'am.

Close examination of the tire tracks shows the victim drove passed the end of your driveway. The victim continued across your backyard, passed the woods, and drove straight into the lake."

"My God!" Mommy exclaimed.

"Where were you folks when this all happened?"

"We were staying at a motel for a couple of days," daddy informed him.

"Which motel were you staying at, Mr. Wellwood?"

"The Lightningville Motor Inn."

"Now let me get this straight. You folks just bought this house, moved in, and already sick of it?" Detective Rosa asked suspiciously.

"Excuse me, Detective Rosa, but you can't possibly expect us to stay here with no heat, water, or electricity. That's why we went to the motel," mommy said flustered.

"I figured that, ma'am."

"So why did you ask, detective?" Daddy wondered.

"Because, I wanted to hear it from you folks."

"Detective Rosa, are we suspects?" Mommy asked.

"No, ma'am, not yet. I just wanna be thorough in my investigation, that's all."

The detective then turned towards the entourage of police officers and medics and told them to pack it up. Detective Rosa then informed my parents that he would keep in touch with them. One by one, they left. First, was the tow truck, carrying the white, "Conservative Power & Gas" van that was pulled from the lake.

Then, the ambulance, carrying Joe, the deceased power representative, left. Last to leave, were the two patrol cars. Detective Rosa was in the last car. Daddy turned towards mommy, shaking his head.

"I don't care what that man says, Heather. We're his prime suspects," daddy declared.

"Did you see the way he was looking at us, dear? It was like he was analyzing everything we said," mommy nervously stated.

"I know. It was like an interrogation," daddy said.

No sooner than the words left his lips, another white van from "Conservative Power & Gas," came up our driveway. The power representative stepped out of the van to greet us.

"Hi, folks! I'm Charlie from Conservative Power & Gas. I'm here to get your lights back on."

"Hello! I'm Michael Wellwood. I'll take you to the back of the house."

Daddy took Charlie, the power rep, to the back of our house, all the time thinking about Detective Rosa. Mommy and daddy were right. Detective Rosa did consider us the prime suspects. What we didn't know was that Charlie, the power rep, was also watching us.

Charlie was best friends with his co-worker, Joe, and he was going to get to the bottom of this, no matter what.

Chapter 7
The Possession of
Michael

Mom and dad were happy to move back into our home again. The electricity was on for the first time in years. When the boiler repairman came and serviced the boiler; heat, and hot and cold water were flowing again. Yes, all seemed peachy for them, but not for me. I still felt that evil presence in the house. Something or someone was watching us. Daddy decided to take another trip up the attic with me. He wanted to finish going through the boxes up there.

"Come on, Samantha! Let's see what other goodies we can find!" Daddy beamed.

"But, daddy?"

"Daddy what? Don't tell me you're still scared of the attic?"

"Uh-huh."

"Oh, come on! There's nothing up there but music boxes, that's all."

"Oh, all right, daddy."

I followed him upstairs to the attic. After awhile of going through some more boxes, we came upon something strange. It was an old wooden chest. The chest was hidden behind the boxes, in the corner. I had a bad feeling about it. Daddy was excited.

"Samantha, look! It looks like an old pirate treasure chest!"

"I-I don't think we should touch it, daddy."

"Oh, honey, there's nothing to be afraid

of. Trust me."

I looked into his warm, trusting eyes and just couldn't refuse. I loved my daddy with all of my heart.

"Oh, all right, daddy."

"Ok, honey. Go downstairs and get me a hammer from my toolbox."

"Ok, daddy." Awhile later, he was banging on the padlock that was on the chest in the attic.

"I've got it!" Daddy exclaimed.

The old wooden chest gave way. The padlock was on the floor. Daddy lifted open the heavy lid.

"Samantha, look!"

The wooden chest was divided into two compartments. The larger compartment held an extra-large, beautiful, hand carved music box. It was much larger than any of the other music boxes we've seen, and much prettier. The mahogany colored wooden music box was about the size of a small suitcase. There were fancy music scroll engravings on it, each one hand-painted in gold. On the top of the lid in the middle of the scrolls, there was an old-fashioned, oval-shaped portrait of a man in a suit, holding a music box. It was Roger Thompson, the creator of the box. The same picture that hung on the wall in the hall, downstairs. Daddy opened the lid of the music box, expecting it to play. Nothing happened.

"I guess it has to be wound, Samantha."

Daddy struggled a bit, getting the wooden music box out of the chest. It was obviously heavy, but he had to take it out to wind it. Daddy found the key in the back and wound it.

"Now, let's see...where's the switch? Here it is!" Daddy said.

Nothing happened. The music box refused to play. Daddy noticed something was missing.

"Hey! The music roll is missing! That's why it won't play."

"Music roll?" I asked him.

"Yeah, the cylinder with the pegs on it. That's where the music is recorded on. Without that, it won't play. Hmm, maybe it's in the other compartment of the chest."

Daddy looked in the smaller compartment on the left of the chest. There was a small, black wooden box. Daddy opened it. Inside, there was a long, golden cylinder with pegs on it and an inscription that read: "He who plays me, shall become me."

"What could that mean, Samantha?"

"I don't know, daddy, but it doesn't sound good."

"Hey, guys! Come down for supper!" Mommy shouted.

"All right, honey! Come on, Samantha, let's leave this here and go eat."

Suddenly, we heard a mysterious voice whisper, "LET ME OUT!"

"What was that?" Daddy asked.

"I don't know daddy, maybe it's just the wind. Please, let's go!"

We went downstairs to eat supper. After we finished supper, daddy took a nap. I helped mommy with the dishes. Then, mommy decided to go to the store to get some dessert.

"You wanna come to the grocery store with me, Samantha?" Mommy asked.

"No, mommy, I'm tired. I think I'll take a nap, too."

"All right, Samantha. I'll be back in a bit."

I waited for mommy to leave, and then I went upstairs to the attic, alone. Scared and nervous, I knew in my gut, that the music box we found was evil. It must not be put together. If daddy completed it, something bad would happen. That was my feeling inside. When I approached the chest, the music box was where we left it. The small black box containing the music roll was empty. Where was the golden music roll? It was just here a while ago. There was a strange glow coming from the music box, it was hypnotic. I stared at the box more closely and noticed something different. Somehow, some way, the missing music roll was now in place! But how? How did this happen? No one here! The music box was now complete and waiting. Waiting for something. But what? It must be destroyed before...

"GO! GO, YOU, BITCH!" The mysterious voice shouted.

I ran down the stairs, scared as hell, slamming the attic stairs shut. Daddy was still sleeping. I stayed near him until mommy came home. It was 1:00 in the morning when I was woken up from a sound sleep, again from that creepy tune and the children singing. This time, much more pronounced. I went to mommy and daddy's room but stopped outside their half-opened door. They were naked in bed. Daddy was on top of mommy, kissing her.

"Mmm, it's been a longgg time, dear," daddy moaned.

"Just be careful, dear. I feel as big as a house with this baby, not very comfortable you know," mommy responded.

Daddy kept kissing mommy on the neck, down to her breasts. A cold draft flew by me and into their room. The music became louder and stronger. Daddy stopped kissing mommy and just froze, like a freeze-frame in a movie.

"Honey? What's the matter, dear? Why'd you stop kissing me?" Mommy asked perplexed.

Daddy's face began to change. He looked like a wild man. Mommy was getting scared and so was I.

"Michael! Michael! Stop it! You're scaring me!"

Suddenly, daddy looked up at her with a twisted expression and said, "The name's Roger, you, bitch! Grrrrrr! C'mere! I ain't had lovin' in a longgg time."

Daddy grabbed mommy's neck. I was scared. I didn't know what to do.

"Michael! Stop it! You're hurting me!"

Suddenly, mommy slapped daddy hard in the face.

"You, son-of-a-bitch! What's gotten into you?!" Mommy screeched.

But that only made daddy angrier.

"You, bitch! I'll kill you!" he said enraged.

Daddy's grip grew tighter around mommy's neck. I could see her gasping for air. I didn't know what else to do, but scream! Mommy looked right at me. Then, she grabbed the telephone on the nightstand and struck daddy square on the head. Daddy collapsed on the floor, unconscious. The cold draft went, along with the music. I ran to my mommy.

"Mommy, mommy! Are you, all right?"

"Yes, baby, I'm ok. I don't know what came over him."

"I told you this house is evil, mommy! I told you!"

"Oh, Samantha. You mustn't think that."

"But it's true! It's true, mommy, I know it."

"I won't believe that. You must not talk

about evil, or you'll invite it into your home."

"But mommy, didn't you hear the music?"

"The music?"

"Something bad always happens here when the music plays," I told her.

"You know, come to think of it, I did hear it. It was that music box tune we've heard before. I just didn't pay it any mind. But the look on your father's face...he was like a crazed man. Then he said his name was Roger. Who the hell is Roger?"

At that moment, daddy began to regain consciousness.

"Ohhhh! My head. What happened? Why am I on the floor?" he asked.

Mommy and I just clung together, not knowing what to do or say.

"Heather, what happened?"

"I honestly don't know, dear. Something came over you...you snapped," mommy said as she began to tremble.

"Whadda ya mean I snapped?"

"You attacked me and I knocked you out!"

"I what?!"

"You went off, Michael! Your own daughter saw you! Look what you did to my neck! Look at it!"

"My God! Did I do that?!" he said horrified at the bruises.

"You tried to kill me, Michael. I-I don't

feel safe around you," mommy stammered.

"Is...this...true, Samantha?"

"Yes, daddy, it is."

"I'm sooo sorry, baby. The last thing I'd ever want to do is hurt either one of you. I love you both so much."

"You don't remember anything?" Mommy asked him.

"All I remember is kissing your neck, and then..."

"And then what, Michael?"

"Well, everything sort of went blank after that...wow, my head really hurts."

"Well, you've got a lump on your head, that's for sure," mommy said with arms crossed around her chest.

"What did you hit me with, dear?" Daddy asked while he still rubbed his head.

"The phone. I hit you with the phone."

"Wow! Very resourceful, dear."

"Michael, I think you should be checked out."

"Checked out? Whadda ya mean checked out?"

"The hospital, Michael. Maybe...maybe, God forbid, you've got a brain tumor or something."

"A brain tumor?! Come on!"

"Michael, you nearly killed me and the baby! You scared the shit out of our daughter! Your own family is afraid of you! Are you listening to me, Michael? You-need-to-be-checked out!"

"Alright, Heather. You win, but can we go first thing in the morning? I'm really tired."

"I think we should go now, Michael."

"I'm tired, dear. I don't feel like hanging around in some waiting room to take a bunch of tests."

"Damnit, Michael! Get your lazy ass up and go to the damn hospital already!"

"I'm tired. We'll do it in the morning."

"Fine. But could you please sleep in the other room until we find out what's wrong with you, Michael? I really don't feel safe around you. Please?"

"Well...all right...I'll go."

"Thank you, dear."

Daddy got up and walked out of the room. Mommy went to lock the bedroom door. She wasn't taking any chances. We tried to sleep, cuddled up together, but all we kept thinking about was daddy. About an hour went by and mommy started to snore. Oh, she would swear she didn't snore. Mommy would say, "You're hearing things. I don't snore." It made me laugh just thinking of that. All of a sudden, out of the blue, the music softly started playing again. I was so scared that I started shaking. Then, I heard footsteps in the hall, followed by the sound of the attic stairs being pulled down. It was daddy. He was going back up in the attic. I decided to wake mommy up.

"Mommy! Mommy! Wake up! Wake up!"

"Whoa, huh? Why'd you wake me up, Samantha?"

"Daddy's up in the attic again!"

"What?" Mommy asked perplexed.

"He's up in the attic and the music's playing again."

"Oh, no! I hear it. Look! Stay here! Ok?"

"Ok, mommy."

Mommy got out of bed and went towards the bedroom door. She slowly unlocked the door and opened it. There were voices coming from the attic, most notably, my father's voice. I snuck right behind my mother until she noticed me.

"I told you to stay in the room," mommy whispered.

"I was scared, mommy."

We stood in the hall, under the attic stairs, listening. The voices were louder and now we could hear daddy talking to someone, but who? There was no one up there, or so we thought.

"YOU MUST TAKE THEM OVER!" the mysterious voice shouted.

"I...must...take...them...over," daddy said in a trance-like tone of voice.

"YES, I'll GET WHAT I DESIRE!

A FAMILY!" the voice shouted again.

"I'll get what I desire, a family!" Daddy repeated.

"COME! I WILL HELP YOU!"

the voice moaned.

At that moment, mommy quickly grabbed the folding attic stairs, and folded them up to the ceiling. Then, she stretched up to hook the padlock on, but mommy couldn't reach it. Daddy was taller than her.

"Shit! I can't reach it! Samantha! Get me the stepping stool from our bedroom! Hurry!"

"Where is it, mommy?"

"It's in the corner by the dresser."

"Ok, mommy!"

I ran to get the stool.

"Let me out! Let me out, you, bitch! I'll kill you!" Daddy roared.

Mommy was stretched to the ceiling, trying to keep the attic stairs from coming down. I finally came back with the stool, but it was too late. Daddy, with super human strength, pushed down the attic stairs, knocking mommy down to the ground. He then jumped on her! I let out a big scream.

"YOU LITTLE BITCH! I'LL GET YOU, TOO!" Daddy snarled.

He looked at me with evil eyes, like souls of hatred. I knew then that this was not my father. Something truly evil had taken over my daddy's body. I threw the stool at his head out of fear for what he would do to mommy and me. He fell to the floor, unconscious. Mommy got up and grabbed me. We hugged for a moment.

"Samantha, grab your coat! We're going to the police!"

"Ok, mommy!" I said as I trembled with fear.

We ran down the stairs, grabbed our coats and headed for the car. Outside, we were greeted by Mr. Bud Smith, the real estate man that sold us this house. What was he doing here this late? Mr. Smith told us to get in his van, so we got in his van and left daddy alone in the house, not knowing if he was alright.

Chapter 8
The Story

Mr. Smith came by in the middle of the night because he had a vision that we were in danger. Mr. Smith started telling us the real story of our house.

"You folks alright?" Mr. Smith asked.

"Yes, Mr. Smith, we're fine. Now, can you please tell us what this is all about? My husband is back there freaking out and I need to know why!" Mommy exclaimed.

"I'm sorry I got you folks inta this, but real estate is ma business. It's ma job to sell houses," Mr. Smith said.

"Mr. Smith, is this really all about our new home?" Mommy asked him.

"Yes, ma'am, I'm afraid so. Look, we're almost at ma office. I'll explain everything to ya's over a cup of coffee, all right?"

"All right, Mr. Smith."

What Mr. Smith didn't realize, was that we were being followed. A car was behind us the whole time, ever since we left our house. I was the only one who noticed it. When we pulled into the driveway of Mr. Smith's office, the strange car that was following us, backed off. It disappeared into the night. We walked into the office and sat down, while Mr. Smith turned on the coffee pot.

"You drink any coffee, girlie?"

"No, thank you, sir."

"Ok, it's just me and your mom then."

"Mr. Smith, please! I need to know what's wrong with our house, and more importantly, my husband."

"All right, Mrs. Wellwood. I'll tell ya the whole story."

"Yes, please do. I'd like ta hear it, too," a voice called out from behind us. The door had been left open. Mr. Smith forgot to close it, and now Charlie, the man that turned on our lights, was standing there.

"Who are you, mister?" Mr. Smith asked.

"My name is Charlie. I followed you people here. I work for 'Conservative Power & Gas.' My best friend and co-worker was killed behind these people's property and I don't think it was an accident."

"All right, sir, you can have a seat, too. Now, let me start at the beginning. The year was 1935. Young Mr. Roger Thompson, who was about 26-years-old at the time, had just finished building his dream house up on Horror Hill. Roger worked real close with the construction folks, he knew what he wanted, ya know. Being a successful inventor and owner of his own company, 'Thompson Music Box Company,' every young woman in town wanted him. Although, Roger was good lookin' too, most of the women were gold diggers, ya know. Anyway, he finally picked one fer his wife. Roger wanted a big family, but after over a year of tryin', he found out that his wife was barren. The doctors said she could **never** have children. This made Roger furious. Oh, ya should have seen the fury in his eyes. Roger felt so cheated, that folks thought he was the one who had killed his wife, although, they could never prove it. Ya see, Roger's wife was found at the bottom of Grace Lake. She apparently drowned. The police became suspicious of Roger, but Roger argued the fact that she always went swimming in the lake. Since the police had no hard evidence against him, they chalked it up as an accident. The townsfolk still believed that Roger Thompson killed his wife and dumped her body in the lake."

"That's where my friend was found, dead in his van," Charlie said to Mr. Smith.

"Yes, I heard about that. I'm sorry fer your loss...anyway, Roger was all alone in that big ole house of his. Tired of bein' alone, he decided ta look fer another wife. The problem was, after what happened to his wife, most women were scared of him. Roger couldn't get a date fer nothin'. He got all bent out of shape and became a recluse...then, somethin' bad happened..."

"What, Mr. Smith?" Mommy asked him.

"Yeah, what happened?" Charlie asked.

"Heh, heh, heh. Easy folks, I'ma tell y'all. But first, time fer some coffee."

"Awwww," we all said in unison.

Mr. Smith got up from his chair and poured coffee for himself, mommy, and Charlie. Then, he sat back down again, to tell us the rest of the story.

"Mmm...coffee's good. Now, let ma see, where was I...?"

"You were saying something bad happened, Mr. Smith," mommy indicated.

"Oh, yeah, that's right. Somethin' really bad happened. All of a sudden, little children started disappearin' from everywhere..."

"Huh? What?" everyone asked.

"Yep. Children disappeared from the school playground, their backyards, and from the park. All in all, over a hunderd kids were missin'. The police, accompanied by frantic parents, searched everywhere, but no one ever found 'em. They just vanished into thin air..." Mr. Smith stated.

"Well, what happened to them, Mr. Smith?" I asked.

"Well, girlie, no one knows fer sure, but some folks suspected Roger Thompson was behind it."

"Mr. Smith, this story is very interesting, but I don't see the connection," mommy interrupted.

"I'm afraid I don't follow what yer sayin', Mrs. Wellwood," Mr. Smith said.

"I'm saying, what does this have to do with us, especially my husband?"

"I'm a gettin' ta that, Mrs. Wellwood. Like I was sayin,' folks became awful suspicious of Mr. Roger Thompson. They started watchin' every move he made. One day, Mrs. Owens, a schoolteacher and parent from the local elementary school, spotted Roger Thompson in the supermarket. Roger was buyin' nothin' but cake, ice cream, and balloons. *What would he be needin' that stuff for?* she thought. Everyone knew he had no family. Mrs. Owens decided ta follow Roger home. When she got there, she pulled out her binoculars that she kept in the glove compartment of her car. Mrs. Owens always carried binoculars with her. She was an avid bird watcher. Then, she saw what she came fer. Children were singing and playing in the backyard, but they looked like they were hypnotized or something. The children were moving in slow motion. Yes, that's what she said, slow motion. As fer their singing, it was more like chanting something or another. Mrs. Owens stared at all the children with her binoculars. Low and behold, she spotted her 6-year-old daughter, Melissa. At that point, Mrs. Owens lost it, so ta speak. She ran towards her daughter callin' out to her. 'Melissa, Melissa!' she shouted. But the girl didn't recognize her. Melissa got scared and ran back in the house. The other children followed her and locked the back door. Mrs. Owens banged and banged on the back door, but the children wouldn't answer. Next thing ya know, Roger Thompson comes out and denies everything. 'You're crazy!' He hollered at her and told her ta leave. When she refused ta go, he waved his hand in front of her and said, 'Forget all you see and go home.' The next thing ya know, she's back in her house. A day later, Mrs. Owens remembered everything. When she told her story to the police, they thought she was crazy. Everything was fine until she mentioned the part about Roger waving his hand in front of her and making her forget everything. But the police still had ta check it out. It was the only lead they had. They sent one patrol car, but when the two officers never called in or returned, more patrol cars were sent. The other police officers found both cops shot dead in front of Mr. Thompson's home. Apparently, the police officers shot each other with their own guns, probably under some sort of hypnotic power from Mr. Thompson."

"Oh, my God!" mommy erupted.

"Man!" Charlie exclaimed.

"Yep! That's how it happened all right. Well, anyway, the other officers weren't takin' any chances. They didn't know what they were up against. So, the police officers busted the door down of ole

Roger's house. What they found still puzzles everyone who remembers it..."

"Well, what did they find, Mr. Smith?" Mommy anxiously asked.

"Yeah, what'd they find, sir?" Charlie reiterated.

"Heh, heh, heh. Y'all are just like little children."

"Oh, come on, Mr. Smith. We have a right to know!"

"Yeah! Come on, Mr. Smith! Spit it out!" Charlie yelled.

"All right, all right. I'll tell ya's. Well, when the cops broke in ta the house, they found ole Roger standin' there, holdin' a great big ole music box. He was chantin' somethin'. The police officers told Roger ta 'drop the box and put yer hands up.' Roger kept on chantin' and started ta glow. Finally, they shot him. The music box began ta glow with him and started playin' this mysterious little tune. I'm sure y'all heard it by now."

"Yes, we have, Mr. Smith. Yes, we have," mommy said.

"Well, anyway, ole Roger dropped the music box as he collapsed on the floor, dyin'. When he dropped it, the music box fell apart. At that moment, both Roger and the music box stopped glowin'. Roger was gone. Funny thing, though..."

"What, Mr. Smith? What?" Mommy eagerly asked him.

"Yeah, what?" Charlie asked.

"Heh, heh, heh. Well, the police officers reported that Roger Thompson didn't just die on the floor. He disintegrated inta thin air. All that was left was his clothes and a pile of dust. Now, most folks would agree that wasn't humanly possible. But the police officers swear they'd seen it right before their eyes."

"Mr. Smith, are you making this up?" Mommy inquired.

"No, ma'am! Honest Ingin'. And believe it or not, there's more."

"More?" Mommy asked with wide eyes.

"Yep! More! It seems those same police officers went searchin' in the house fer the missin' children. In the basement, they found piles of the children's clothes, with piles of dust, but no children. Legend has it, that Roger took the children with him, wherever that was."

"Oh, come on now, Mr. Smith. You expect us to believe such hogwash?" Charlie chuckled.

"Really, Mr. Smith. Come on," mommy laughed.

"Why, it's the truth I tell ya! Four police officers said the same damn thing. Here! Let me show ya's."

Mr. Smith opened up his desk draw and pulled out some newspaper clippings. None of us could believe our eyes, especially when we were looking at the pictures of the remains of Roger Thompson and the children. It was just like Mr. Smith said, nothing left but piles of clothes and dust.

"Mr. Smith, that really is hard to swallow. So, what happened next? I'm afraid to ask," mommy said with a shiver.

"Well, bein' that ole Roger Thompson had no family ta pass the house down ta, the town took it over. Someone's gotta pay the property taxes on it, ya know. Anyway, the head of the town hall at the time, Miss Gloria Hacket, took charge of cleaning the house up, and puttin' it on the market. Miss Hacket firmly believed that Roger Thompson was a male witch!" Mr. Smith exclaimed.

"Huh? What?" we all said in disbelief.

"That's right! Warlock! That's what she called him, warlock!"

"Well, Mr. Smith, how would she know that?" Mommy asked.

"Heh, heh, heh. Easy. That ole bitch looked like a frickin' witch, herself," Mr. Smith busted out laughing.

"Mr. Smith! Please!" Mommy scolded him.

"Oh, I'm sorry about the cussin', ma'am. I guess I got carried away," Mr. Smith said with a shrug.

"Yes, please, Mr. Smith. I have my daughter with me."

"Alright, ma'am, I'm a keep it clean fer

ya. Anyway, Miss Gloria Hacket claimed that *she* believed in the supernatural powers herself. Miss Hacket became obsessed with Roger and all his belongins. Even ta the point of livin' in his house fer awhile. Miss Hacket was never married and was considered a loner, herself. After about a year, the house was finally put up fer sale. Although, the original furniture that belonged ta the Thompsons was left in the house ta make it more marketable, no one was interested in buyin' it. The town spent money updatin' it, lowerin' the price and everythin'. No one wanted it. No one, until you out-a-town folks bought it."

"Yes, and I'm sorry we did, Mr. Smith. You weren't all that truthful with us, were you?" Mommy indicated.

"Again, I'm sorry, ma'am. Oh! There's just one more thing I forgot ta mention."

"What's that, Mr. Smith? I can't bear anymore," mommy sighed.

"Well, Miss Gloria Hacket made it a point ta keep Roger Thompson's music box separated. She placed it in a chest and kept it locked up in his attic. A murderer's music box, that's what she called it, a murderer's music box. She firmly believed that if the music box were assembled, ole Roger's spirit would come back with a vengeance. Now, the way I see it, everything should be fine, as long as ya keep that old music box apart and locked up in the attic."

"Mr. Smith!" I cried.

"Eh, what is it, girlie?"

"I'm afraid it's too late for that," I said with slumped shoulders.

"Huh? What?" Everyone asked.

"Oh, honey, what are you saying?" mommy asked as she grabbed me.

"Well, me and daddy found that chest and daddy started putting it together."

"Aw, shit!" Mr. Smith exclaimed.

"Mr. Smith!" mommy yelled at him again.

"I'm sorry, ma'am. Now, lemme get this straight. Y'all busted the locks, went up in that ole attic, found the music box, and put it together?" he asked.

"Well, not exactly, sir. Daddy started to put it together, but mommy called us down for supper. I went back up later and found it all put together and glowing. After that, daddy started acting weird. I'm sorry, mommy. Daddy really wanted to put it together."

"Oh, honey, it's all right. What's done is done. Mr. Smith, what do we do now? Can we talk to Miss Hacket and see if she can help us?" mommy asked.

"I'm afraid not, ma'am. Miss Hacket passed away over 10 years ago. All I can say is this: get back up in that attic, destroy the music box, and hopefully your husband will come back to ya."

After that, Mr. Smith drove us back to the house and told us to be careful. Mr. Smith also gave us a gun, just in case.

Chapter 9
A Phantom's Demise

Mr. Smith had just pulled into our driveway, but me and mommy were scared to get out of his car.

"Look folks, I know yer scared and all, but it'll be alright. I done gave ya the gun fer protection."

"Oh, Mr. Smith, me and my daughter would sure feel safer if *you* came inside with us. Please?"

"I'm sorry, ma'am, but this is somethin' yer gonna have ta do. After all, he's yer husband. Maybe you can reason with him. Maybe you can get him ta force ole Roger's spirit outta his body. Maybe..."

"That's a lot of maybes, Mr. Smith," mommy said discouraged.

"Look, I'ma sit here in ma van. That's the best I can do fer you's, all right?"

"But, Mr. Smith, please!" Mommy pleaded.

"I'm sorry, Mrs. Wellwood, but that's the best I can do. I'll be here for a while. If ya need help, just give a holler, all right?"

"All right, Mr. Smith. Guess we'll just have to have it your way. Come on, Samantha, let's go," mommy said with a cry in her voice.

"But, MOM!"

"Let's go!" She exclaimed.

"All right, mommy."

We left Mr. Smith in the van and headed for the front door. Then, we heard the most blood-curdling scream you could ever imagine. We turned around to find it was Mr. Smith.

"NO! NO! HELP! I brought them back fer ya! NOOOO!" Mr. Smith screamed in agony.

"YOU FAILED ME FOR THE LAST TIME!" Roger's spirit yelled.

"N-O-O!" Mr. Smith cried. Roger's ghost was engulfing poor Mr. Smith and his van.

"NOOO! Give me another chance! PLEASE!" Mr. Smith begged.

"DIE MOTHERFUCKER! BURN IN HELL!" Roger erupted.

"NOOOO!" Mr. Smith screeched.

Mr. Smith was being burned alive in his own van by Roger Thompson's ghost. Just then, the van blew up! We heard the sounds of glass shattering and the final cries of a man whose life had been stolen from him in less than a heartbeat. It was the most horrifying thing we had ever seen and heard. I will never forget it.

"YOU'RE NEXT, BITCHES!" the spirit's voice shouted.

At that moment, the giant ghostly face of Roger Thompson appeared from the flames. It was floating towards us. Mommy had unlocked the front door and grabbed my hand.

"Hurry, Samantha, inside!"

Mommy slammed the door shut and locked it. It was cold and dark in the house, so cold, that our breaths looked like smoke coming out of our mouths.

"Shit! It's cold in here. The heat must be off. Where's the damn light switch? Oh, here it is. Shit! The electricity's out again," mommy said disheartened.

All of a sudden, Roger's music box started playing again. The music was so loud and deafening, that it sounded like a big stereo system turned all the way up.

"Mommy, I'm scared!"

Mommy opened up her purse. She took out her flashlight and put the gun, that Mr. Smith gave her, in her coat pocket.

"Come on, Samantha! Let's find that damn music box and destroy it before it's too late."

"But mommy, what about daddy?"

"I have a feeling he'll find us, first. Sweetheart, we've got to be extra careful, you know. Your father isn't really your father. He's possessed by that frickin' ghost."

"I know, mommy," I said with a shudder.

Mommy turned towards the painting of Roger Thompson on the wall.

"And as for you, you son-of-a-bitch...take that!" she said as she began to smash the portrait of Roger. "I hate you! I hate you! You son-of-a-bitch! Leave us alone!" she screamed hyperventilating.

Mommy smashed and tore up Roger Thompson's picture. A low moan came from the painting, like it was crying out in pain, and then, the music just stopped.

"I'm sorry, honey. I guess I just lost it. Come on, let's go," mommy said quietly.

We headed upstairs, not knowing what we would find. We looked in all of the rooms upstairs. There was no sign of daddy. Suddenly, the attic stairs started coming down by themselves. Mommy's flashlight was getting dim.

"Shit! My flashlight batteries are going. I wish the lights would come back on," mommy whined.

"Me too, mommy. I'm scared."

Then, at that very moment, as if our wishes were granted, the lights came back on. We both looked up at the attic stairs, waiting to see if anyone was coming down. No one came.

"Samantha. You stay down here and keep a lookout while I go upstairs."

"But, I wanna go with you, mommy."
"Please. Do as I say, all right?"

"All right, mommy, but please hurry."
"I'll try."

Mommy cautiously went up the attic stairs while I stayed at the bottom. Although there was a pull chain light up there, she kept her flashlight in her hand, just in case. Mommy walked around up in the attic, looking for daddy and the music box. Then, she came back to the top of the stairs and called me.

"Samantha! Come here."

"Yes, mommy?"

"Come up here. It's all right."

"Ok, mommy."

I climbed up the stairs to meet her.

"I don't know how those stairs came down. There's no one here. It must be one of Thompson's tricks. Anyway, where did you say that music box was?"

"It was over there, mommy, near that old chest."

"The chest was empty, and I don't see anything except those boxes," mommy indicated.

"But, it was there, mommy. I swear!"

"All right then, help me look for it."

We searched and searched everywhere in that attic. We even looked into some of the boxes that were big enough to hold that very large and special music box. It was nowhere to be found. We were both frustrated.

"Well, that does it. We've been up here for over three hours, Samantha, and nothing."

"But, where could it be, mommy?"

"The only other explanation is..."

"Daddy?"

"I'm afraid so. Your father has it."

"Well, what'll we do, mommy?"

"I don't know, honey, but one thing's for sure..."

"What's that, mommy?"

"We have got to get that music box from him and destroy it before it's too late. We might as well go back downstairs and look for him," she said with a sigh.

"Mommy?"

"What, honey?"

"You're not going to shoot daddy with Mr. Smith's gun, are you?"

"Oh, honey, that's the last thing I want to do. I love your father very much, but we do have another one to consider, you know."

"Who, mommy?"

"Why the baby, of course! Your future sister! She'll be due in less than a month."

"How do you know it's gonna be a girl, mommy?"

"Easy! I had an ultrasound test done a while ago. The doctor told me it's a girl. He even showed me a picture of her on his machine."

"Wow! Does daddy know?"

"Sure! He was with me when I had the test."

"Well, how come no one ever told me?"

"Because we wanted to surprise you, Samantha," daddy's voice suddenly rang out.

Daddy was standing at the bottom of the attic stairs, looking up at us.

"Daddy!"

"Michael! You startled us."

"Really?" Daddy asked inquisitively.

"Yes, really," mommy said in a suspicious tone.

Daddy seemed himself again, but mommy wasn't taking any chances. She had her hand in her coat pocket, on the gun, all along.

"How long were you standing there, Michael?"

"Long enough to hear you reminisce to our daughter. You two coming down or what?" Daddy asked cheerfully.

"Well, I..." mommy said hesitantly.

"Come on, dear. Can't you see I'm all right?"

"All right, Michael, we're coming down. Come on, Samantha."

Mommy went down the attic stairs and I followed closely behind her.

"So, what were you two doing up there? Looking for something?"

"Yes. I mean no," mommy said trembling.

"Yes, no. Which is it? Hmm, I mean, you seem confused, dear," he said to her gently.

"I guess I'm just a little nervous, that's all."

"Nervous?" he innocently asked.

"Yes, nervous. Well, let's face it, Michael. You were nothing short of being a monster, and now you show up here like everything's ok. How the **hell** do you expect me to react?!"

mommy cried hysterically.

She broke down and cried on daddy's shoulder. Daddy gave mommy a hug.

"I'm so sorry, baby. I was sick, but now I'm better. I didn't mean to hurt you, honest. I love you. Come, let's talk in our bedroom."

We followed daddy into the master bedroom.

"But...how...do...I...know...for sure?"

"This is how, baby."

They looked into each other's eyes and tenderly kissed. It was a long, intense kiss. You could still tell that they loved each other very much. Then, all of a sudden, mommy withdrew from him...

"You're not my husband. I don't know who the hell you are, but you're not my husband!"

"You're very good, aren't you, baby? You know who I am, don't you? Ha, ha, ha, ha!" daddy laughed maliciously.

"Then, you are for real, aren't you, Roger?"

"In the flesh. As real as ever. Ha, ha, ha, ha!"

"What have you done with my husband?"

"Oh, he's here safe inside with me...for now...until I'm done with him. Ha, ha, ha, ha!"

"Michael! Michael! Listen to me! You've got to fight him!"

mommy exclaimed in desperation.

Daddy, with help from Roger's spirit, slapped mommy so hard that she fell to the floor.

"Ha, Ha, ha! You're no match for me, baby!" he snarled.

"YOU SON-OF-A-BITCH! YOU'VE HURT OUR BABY!" mommy screamed.

"FUCK YOU! I'M TIRED OF THIS SHIT! I'M NOT BEING CHEATED AGAIN!" daddy and Roger growled.

"LEAVE MY MOMMY ALONE!"

"Well, will ya looky here?! If it isn't little 'Miss Sissy-Ass Mary.' Leave my mommy alone," he mocked me. "Oooo, I'm so scared," he continued laughing.

"You leave my daughter alone! D'ya hear me, Thompson?! We know all about you, and **YOU'LL NEVER HAVE US!"**

"Is that so? Ha, ha, ha! Well, I may not be able to control you two, but I'll have your unborn child," daddy sinisterly smiled.

"NEVER, YOU BASTARD!" mommy tearfully shouted.

"Never say never, bitch. I'll soon have what's rightfully mine."

"Over my dead body," mommy said through clenched teeth.

"Oh! That could be arranged. Now, enough talking. **GIVE ME THE FUCKING BABY!"**

Daddy, with the help of Roger

Thompson's spirit, waved his hands at mommy while she was still on the floor. Suddenly, mommy looked like she was in pain. Mommy began screaming. Then, daddy waved his hands in up and down, slicing motions. Suddenly, cuts were made on mommy's belly, right through what was left of her white blouse! She screamed in misery. There was blood all over her stomach. She looked like a torn rag doll, pinned to the floor.

"COME TO ME! COME TO ME, MY CHILD!"

Mommy's belly was starting to split open through her new wounds. She was in agony. I felt so helpless, not knowing what to do while time was running short. I took a look around the room, searching, searching for something, anything that could help. Then, I saw it, partially covered up with clothes in the corner, the music box we were looking for! Daddy, or should I say Roger, was trying to hide it from us. He knew all along we were looking for it. By now, you could see more blood, guts, and part of the baby coming through mommy's belly. Roger was doing his best to extract the baby from mommy's belly. I knew I had to act fast. I started to run across the room towards the music box.

"NO! NOT SO FAST YOU LITTLE BITCH!"

Roger looked at me and waved his hand. I was thrown back to where I was without him even touching me! He was very powerful. Suddenly, two shots rang out!

"DIE, YOU-SON-OF-A-BITCH!" mommy yelled.

"OW! FUCK!" daddy and Roger screeched.

Mommy had shot daddy while he was distracted by me. Daddy and Roger were both going down on the floor.

"FUCK! MY NEW BODY! It hurts..." daddy and Roger moaned.

Roger's spirit was trying to emerge from daddy's dying body. With no time to lose, I decided to make a quick dash across the room. Then, I quickly uncovered the music box and grabbed it. By now, Roger's spirit had completely emerged from my daddy's limp body and was heading straight towards me.

"NO! NO, YOU, BITCH! GIVE IT TO ME! GIVE IT TO ME!"

Without even thinking, as big and heavy as it was, I picked the music box up high above my head.

"NO! GIVE IT TO ME!"

Before the phantom got within arm's reach of me, I threw the music box out towards the bedroom window.

"NOOOOO!" Roger screeched.

Roger Thompson's spirit started to

disintegrate. I looked out of the broken bedroom window. There, on the driveway, in a million pieces, with broken glass all around, was all that was left of it. Roger Thompson's precious music box was destroyed, and so was his ghost.

No more music. No more hell. Suddenly, the house started shaking. It was also getting very warm. I went over to where daddy was lying. He had two bloody chest wounds from the bullets. Daddy was not breathing, he was gone. I kissed his forehead and cried hysterically. The house was shaking more intensely now and it was getting hot. I didn't know what was happening. I tried to get myself together. Then, I went to where mommy was. Mommy was lying in a big pool of blood on the floor. The gun was still in her hand. Her baby was partially exposed from her bludgeoned belly. They were both gone. I started crying again.

Roger Thompson had taken away my whole family. Now, I was all alone. The house started coming apart. Windows were smashing. A fire had broken out in the attic. The flames were coming through the attic stairwell in the hall. Roger Thompson was gone, and he was taking his house with him. I knew I had to get out of the house before it was too late for me. The house was crumbling and burning. It felt like an earthquake and a fire at the same time. I ran out of the master bedroom, into the hall, and down the stairs. The flames were following me. Everything in the house was falling apart. Walls and ceilings were crumbling and coming down. There was glass from the broken windows everywhere! I finally made it to the front door. I opened the door and ran outside, watching the house burn down to the ground, and thinking about the bodies of my mother and father, burning with it...thinking about Roger Thompson...thinking about all of those beautiful music boxes up in the attic burning, too. Thinking, and worrying. I wondered, who will take care of me, and where will I go?

Chapter 10
Please Don't Take Me Back

"I was sitting in the police station being grilled like a porterhouse steak. Detective Rosa at the precinct kept asking me the same questions over and over again. 'Did I set the fire?' 'How was it started?' 'Who was in the house?' 'Why was I outside?' Over and over he asked. Then, he rephrased the questions until finally, I just broke down and cried. Tomorrow was going to be my 13th birthday. No one cared, not even myself. So, that's my story, sir."

"I see! That's some story," said a male British motel clerk.

"Do you think you can help me out, Mister? I really need a place to stay. I don't have any money, but I'm willing to work for you."

"I'm sorry, I didn't quite catch your name Miss..." the motel clerk said.

"Wellwood. Samantha Wellwood."

"Well, Miss Wellwood, let me see what I can do for you."

"Thank you, sir. I'd appreciate it..."

I hope he gets me a room fast. Gee, I wonder who he's calling on the phone? Shouldn't he just ask the bellhop? Maybe, I'll get the same room I was in with mommy and daddy, years ago, when I was little. He's been on that phone a long time. I wish I could hear what he's saying. Damn! What's taking so long? He keeps looking at me while he's talking on the phone. If it wasn't for this stupid counter and window separating us, I'd hear what he was saying, and maybe to whom he was talking to...well, finally he hung up that phone. Now, maybe I can get some service around here. It's not nice to keep a girl waiting, you know. Here he comes...

"Miss Wellwood. I have someone coming here to help you out. He should be here shortly."

"Excuse me, sir, I'm afraid I don't understand. I asked *you* for help. I need a place to stay. Now you're sending me elsewhere? How dare you! I'm not a charity case!"

"Miss Wellwood, please! I assure you, this person could help..."

"Help? I believe I was asking *you* for that!"

"Look, dearie, it's just that your story seems, rather, shall we say, far-fetched?"

"Far-fetched?! How rude! Everything I've told you was real!"

"Really?"

"Yes, really! Now, I don't know or even care who this other person is. I only want to deal with you."

"But, Miss Wellwood..."

"Sir! Like I was saying, I'm **NOT** a charity case. I need a place to stay and I'm willing to work for it, right here in the Lightningville Motor Inn."

"But, Miss Wellwood...excuse me, did

you say, Lightningville Motor Inn?"

"Yes, that's right! Right here in the Lightningville Motor Inn."

"You think that...oh, that's rich!" the motel clerk laughed hysterically.

"What the **HELL** is so damn funny!"

"My word, you really had me going, lassie. You're even sicker than they say you are!"

"And just, what the hell do you mean by that remark?!"

"Miss Wellwood, what I mean is that you have quite an imagination. A most vivid one at that."

"How dare you?!" "Miss Wellwood. You are in the Light Hill Motor Inn, in the town of Light Hill."

"No! Lightningville!"

"My dear, Miss Wellwood, there's no such place as Lightningville, at least, not around here."

"NO, NO, YOU'RE WRONG! It's Lightningville. I know it!"

"Oh, Miss Wellwood. Here! Let me show you something. Isn't this you on the cover of the Sunday newspaper? It says here, you escaped from the Light Hill Insane Asylum; although, they have you listed under another name. That *is* you, isn't it?"

"NO! NO! It isn't!"

"Dearie, I've spoken to your doctor, he's on his way."

"NO! How could you?! I trusted you! I

trus-..."

"Miss Wellwood! Miss Heather Wellwood!" a voice called out.

"Huh? Who are you?"

"It's me! Dr. Lawrence! I've come to take you back!"

"NO! I don't know who you are and I'm not going with you."

"Oh, you know who I am. I'm your psychiatrist. It's time to go back to Light Hill."

"NO! NO! Please don't take me back! I want to stay here in Lightningville with my family."

"Oh, Miss Wellwood. Please don't make this any more difficult than it already is."

"No, please! I'm Samantha!"

"Samantha's gone! Look! We've been through this over and over for the past 10 years. There is no Lightningville and your family is dead. You've killed them."

"LIES! LIES! They're all nothing but lies!"

"Excuse me, doctor, may I interject?" the clerk asked.

"Sure, sir, and thank you for calling us, Mr. Henderson."

"No problem, doctor. Anyway, this all seems so familiar. I started to believe her rather lengthy and quite vivid story. But, when I went over to our guest book to see what I could do for her, I noticed her picture on the cover of the newspaper.

Doctor, before I called you, I remembered *something* of her story. It was all so long ago, you know. Could you please enlighten me? After all, I do feel partially responsible for her."

"Well, I understand your concern for her, sir, but I'm afraid I can't divulge any more information than the newspapers. You know, doctor-patient confidentiality."

"Yes, yes, I know," Mr. Henderson, the motel clerk, stated.

"Anyway, her name is Heather Wellwood. She moved up here with her then husband, Michael. That was in 1985. 10 years ago. At that time, she was pregnant. Although Heather claimed she moved up here for a better way of life for her budding family, there was another reason. Heather and Michael Wellwood bought that old house up on Harough Hill..."

"It was Horror Hill!" Heather retaliated.

"Miss Wellwood, please! Anyway, everything was going all right until one day, she came home early from work. Heather walked in the house quietly. She wanted to surprise her husband. While she was inside the house, Heather heard moans and grunting. One voice was her husband, Michael, and the other was another woman. Heather snuck up the stairs and found her husband, in bed, making love to her ex-friend and neighbor,

Maria."

"Maria! That bitch! I hope she rots in HELL!" Heather said enraged.

"My word. Is that what set her off, doctor?" Mr. Henderson asked.

"Yes, I'm afraid so."

"That bitch was riding my husband like a horse!"

"I know you're upset, Heather, but you've got to put the past behind and move on."

"So, doctor, what happened next?" Mr. Henderson asked intrigued.

"Well, after catching her husband in bed with Maria, Heather became distraught. She needed to seek revenge, and she did. Heather quietly went back down the stairs. She went to the garage and got a full can of gas. Heather poured gasoline in and around the whole house, lit a match, and set it ablaze. The old house went up like a torch. Heather was outside, watching it burn, listening to them scream in agony. They never had a chance. By the time the fire department got there, it was all too late for Michael and Maria."

"Oh, my God! Those poor people. Burned alive!" Mr. Henderson said in horror.

"The hell with them! They got what they deserved."

"Oh, Heather...anyway, Heather felt

guilty. She broke down and cried. But before the fire department arrived, Heather ran to her car and drove off. By now, Heather was hysterical. She didn't see the big oak tree up ahead. Heather crashed into the tree. She was taken to the hospital's emergency room with serious injuries. They tried to save her baby, but with all that blood loss, Samantha didn't make it."

"My poor baby. They showed her to me, all covered in blood," Heather sobbed.

"I see! So, Samantha was her unborn, or shall I say, still-born child," Mr. Henderson indicated.

"That's right. When Heather found out her baby was going to be a girl, she named her after her late twin sister, Samantha."

"I'm sorry, did you say late twin sister?" Mr. Henderson asked incredulously.

"Yes, that's right. Heather and her twin sister were riding their bicycles, when out of nowhere, a car came speeding around the corner. It was a drunk driver. The car struck and killed Samantha, right in front of Heather. Samantha was almost 13 when she died."

"Good Lord! What a terrible thing for a child to endure!" Mr. Henderson stated in sorrow.

"Yes, I know."

"Huh, such trauma...but there's still one other thing that puzzles me, doctor."

"What's that, Mr. Henderson?"

"Well, earlier, you spoke of the real reason that Heather and her husband moved up here. Why on earth would anyone want to leave all the conveniences of the city with public transportation and all, just to come all the way up here?"

"Well, Mr. Henderson, for one thing, to get away from the other woman."

"The other woman, Dr. Lawrence?"

"The other woman, Mr. Henderson, was Maria Santos. You see, Heather suspected her husband was cheating on her, with Maria, for a long time. She even caught them in the park kissing."

"That bitch! She stole my husband!" Heather exclaimed.

"Good Lord!" Mr. Henderson said.

"Heather! You need to calm down...as I was saying, Mr. Henderson, Heather knew all along of her husband and Maria. So, she convinced her husband that moving up here would be better for them and the baby. Heather never confronted her husband about Maria. She thought that moving far away from the problem would solve it. Of course, Michael, her husband, had other plans. Michael planned to bring Maria up to the house while his wife was at work. Heather had grown more suspicious of her husband when he decided to buy another used car. Michael worked from home and the grocery store was less than a mile walk if he needed anything before she got home. With the bills slowly piling up, the last thing the Wellwoods needed was another car with the loan to go along with it, but Michael was very adamant about getting a second car. Heather argued that there was nothing wrong with the 'good ole reliable' car that they had. However, Michael still wanted another car, 'a backup,' he said, just in case. So, Heather finally gave in. A day after they got the second car, Heather decided to come home early from work. That was the day she caught her husband in bed with Maria Santos, and that was the day she set fire to the house, killing them both."

"I'm sorry! But they deserved it!" Heather sobbed.

"Now I remember that story. It was in the papers, the tele, and the radio. All about this crazy, jealous woman that set her house ablaze, killing her husband and his lover. It was all so long ago. She was supposed to get life imprisonment, but instead, they found her insane."

"Yes, that's correct, Mr. Henderson... Heather! It's time to go back,"
Dr. Lawrence declared.

"NO! You can't make me!" Heather snapped.

"I assure you I can, Miss Wellwood. I've brought Officer O' Mallory with me. He's waiting just outside of the front door. Now, I don't want to see you get hurt, Heather. Please, let's go," Dr. Lawrence calmly stated.

"No! Not this time! Back off! Or I'll…"

"Heather! Where did you get that gun?!" Dr. Lawrence asked frightened.

"I found it at the corner of the counter."

"My word! That's me gun! I was just loading it! Just in case. I'm sorry, Dr. Lawrence. I was interrupted by Miss Wellwood and I guess I just forgot to put it away," Mr. Henderson stated.

"That's water under the bridge now, Mr. Henderson. Now, Heather! Don't make this any harder! Give me the gun!"

"No! Never!" Heather cried.

"Give me the gun! Please!" Dr. Lawrence shouted.

"No! Back off or I'll shoot!"

"Heather! Please! Give me the…"

Suddenly, a shot rang out.

"Oh God! My heart!" Dr. Lawrence exclaimed as he fell to the ground with a thud.

"Good Lord! You've killed him!" Mr. Henderson cried.

"Back off or you're next!" Heather shouted as the tears streamed down her face.

"Oh God, no!" Mr. Henderson yelped.

"Now, I'm getting out of here! Do you understand?"

"Yes! Yes! Of course! Just don't shoot me, please!" Mr. Henderson pleaded.

Heather ran outside, but Officer O' Mallory caught up with her.

"FREEZE LADY!" he shouted.

"OFFICER! SHE'S GOT A GUN!" Mr. Henderson said frantically.

"ALL RIGHT! DROP IT, LASSIE!" Officer O' Mallory shouted.

"NO! I'M NOT GOING BACK!" Heather responded. "I WARN YA! I'LL NOT FAIL TA SHOOT!" Officer O' Mallory indicated.

"NEVER!"

"DROP THE GUN, LAS!"

"NO! I'M NOT GOING BACK!"

"I SAID DROP IT!"

"NOOO!"

Just then, Officer O' Mallory opened fire on Heather Wellwood. Two shots rang out followed by her screaming and sputtering up blood. Finally, she collapsed to the ground.

"You've killed her! You've killed her, officer." Mr. Henderson said in disbelief.

"You saw her, laddie! She was going ta shoot me! Self-defense, that's what it was. Self-defense."

"Good Lord! So much blood, right in front of me. In me own motel. So much blood. So much blood. So much blood......"

· ·

"Ah, a very interesting story, Mr..."

"Henderson, sir. Henry Henderson. And you?"

"I am Sheik Abdul Jermol. Now, let's talk business. How much did you say you wanted for this motel?"

"My price, Mr. Jermol, is a steal. Only $1,500,000."

"$1,500,000?"

"Yes, that's correct. "$1,500,000."

"Mr. Henderson. Your price seems a bit excessive, wouldn't you say?"

"My price is more than fair, sir. This place is a genuine gold mine, a moneymaker."

"Then, why do you want to sell it?"

"Frankly, I'm getting too old for this rubbish. You know, keeping the customers happy, the cleaning and maintenance. I want to leave America, go back home to England, and retire."

"Yes, I understand. But "$1,500,000...""

"You'll make much more than that before the year is out. I can assure you. The townspeople have made this motel sort of a national landmark. See this brochure? Why they've nicknamed this place, 'The Haunted Light Hill Motor Inn.' Why, it's a tourist attraction. People come from everywhere to see the ghosts of Dr. Lawrence and Heather Wellwood. They were both shot and killed right here in this lobby, on that very same floor.

Their spirits never rest. Every night at approximately 11:30, their ghosts come out. Why this place is packed! All of our rooms are full. In about five minutes, all of our guests will come down to see the ghosts."

"Why do they come out at 11:30, Mr. Henderson?"

"Because, that was the time they were both shot and killed, Mr. Jermol. Look! Our guests are coming down already! The lobby is filling up!"

"That's a very impressive amount of people, Mr. Henderson! And this happens every night?"

"Yes! Every night!"

Suddenly, a mysterious sound erupted through the halls of the lobby.

"What was that, Mr. Henderson?"

"It's them! They're here."

"Heather. HEATHER! Come with meee..." the spirit of Dr. Lawrence cried out.

"NOOOO! YOU CAN'T MAKE ME!" Heather's spirit moaned in distress.

The crowd was awed. They couldn't believe what was taking place before their eyes!

"Very impressive display, Mr. Henderson!" the sheik yelled amongst the shattered glass and screaming.

"Yes, I know. It's been going on every night, for nearly 25 years,"

Mr. Henderson stated.

"Nearly 25 years?"

"Yes, since 1995, when they passed on.

"Mr. Henderson, you've got yourself a deal."

"I say, mate, jolly good show! Let's go sign the papers."

"Ah, just one question, Mr. Henderson."

"What's that, mate?"

"What ever happened to the house that burned down on Harough Hill?"

"A wealthy young couple bought it a few years ago and restored it. Thompson, that's who it was. Roger and Thelma Thompson..."

~THE END~

If you found this book to be a riveting, hair-raising ride, then you're going to love our fully dramatized audio movie in audio book format available at:
Amazon.com
And for download on Audible.com

Theme from "A Murderer's Music Box" by Manuel Rose is available at:
CDBaby.com

Published by MMRproductions.com
815 Route 82 # 51
Hopewell Junction, New York 12533

About The Authors

Manuel "Manny" Rose (1960-), born in Brooklyn, New York, is the owner and CEO of MMRproductions.com and MyChildStorytime.com. He started his own business in 2000, which has evolved and branched out into multiple avenues, including how-to educational products. As a professional audio/video producer, writer, singer and voice actor, he provided the screenwriting and narration for the instructional films he produced, as well as character voice-overs for his new line of children's audio stories, including his latest project: "My Child Storytime VOL. 1," which is a CD that features all original stories and songs. He is currently working on several other children's stories as well as other adult thrillers. Manny is also a proud member of ASCAP and the Dutchess County Regional Chamber of Commerce.

Please Visit My Websites At:

MyChildStorytime.com and MMRproductions.com

Melissa Rose (1991-), born in Wappingers Falls, New York, is the partner, editor, and production assistant of MMRproductions.com and MyChildStorytime.com. In 2013, she graduated summa cum laude from SUNY New Paltz with her Bachelor of Arts degree in English, and a concentration in creative writing. She has been writing short stories, poems, and songs since she was a young child. Although much of her work is currently unpublished, she has several copyrighted songs that she has written and recorded herself, and she is a proud member of ASCAP. She hopes to record and produce an album of her own work soon.

Books, audio books and theme music soundtrack can be ordered.
For information please write to:
MMRproductions.com
815 Route 82 # 51
Hopewell Junction, New York 12533

Visit Manuel Rose at:

https://www.goodreads.com/author/show/17650713.
Manuel_Rose